Willow's Dawn

GoldieAnn S. Brand

Copyright © 2020 GoldieAnn S. Brand

All rights reserved.

ISBN: 9798643767152

DEDICATION

For my family

CONTENTS

PROLOGUE	PAGE 1
CHAPTER ONE	PAGE 8
CHAPTER TWO	PAGE 16
CHAPTER THREE	PAGE 21
CHAPTER FOUR	PAGE 27
CHAPTER FIVE	PAGE 31
CHAPTER SIX	PAGE 38
CHAPTER SEVEN	PAGE 43
CHAPTER EIGHT	PAGE 48
CHAPTER NINE	PAGE 54
CHAPTER TEN	PAGE 60
EPILOGUE	PAGE 71

ACKNOWLEDGMENTS

Thank you to my Editor Diana for a job well done,
and to Stefan Keller for the beautiful artwork that is my cover.

PROLOGUE

Twenty Years Ago
A young girl named Jenny spun wildly in the breeze. She loved hearing them laugh and cheer. Oh, how she loved them both. She could smell the salt coming off of the water and the flower beds that lined the white wrap-around porch of her grandparent's plantation home. The combination of the two was a smell that made her happy, a smell that meant she was safe. Jenny could hear her grandmother telling her to be careful, calling out to her that she was too close to the edge. But that didn't stop her. She was having too much fun. She was spinning so fast she was becoming dizzy. Jenny decided to stop and rest, but she couldn't. Something was telling her to keep going, keep spinning, and keep laughing. She was getting scared as she lost all sense of control. She wanted to cry out, but something was controlling her. Why couldn't anyone see? Why didn't her grandparents help her? She opened her eyes to find them both, but all she could see was him. She felt his hands shove her forward. She lost her already precarious balance and fell off the edge of the cliff. Right before she blacked out, she focused on his face. The face she loved so much had now become her betrayer.

***

You could hear the police sirens from every corner of the quiet, quaint town. Everyone knew something horrifying had finally happened at Willow's Dawn, the old Victorian mansion on the cliff, but even now they all looked the other way. The Setliffs had once been pillars of the community, but in the past few years, something had changed. No one knew what had happened, nor did they care to know anything about the Setliff's and their menacing house. For the last three weeks, the Setliff's had been wholly shunned, ridiculed, and made invisible to the rest of the town. *Maybe whatever has transpired is for the best,* you could hear the natives whisper.

A massive storm was raging fearlessly that night. It was like a bull trying to break free from its cage: never-ending and relentless. A young man pulled his police car up the long, winding driveway and came to a halt near the end. He stepped out of his car, took a deep and powerful breath, and looked towards the house. There she was, Willow's Dawn, just as beautiful as she was eerie. He watched as the lighting played chase along her windows sills, looking just as terrifying as she did welcoming. *Never did I think I would see such a case this early in my career, let alone in this town,* he thought. He tried to shield his face from the cold rain as it hammered him like nails. He shut the car door and walked up the steps in his bright yellow slicker. He reached into his inner pocket with trembling hands and pulled out a small notebook.

Jonathan Riley extended his hand to the man now in front of him while looking him up and down. He was an older gentleman, maybe in his fifties, with lines darting out away from his eyes and frown marks around his mouth. He had never understood why they were called laugh lines when it left you looking like such a sourpuss. *Maybe it comes from years of being on the force. Will that be me in thirty years?* he considered.

"Hello. I'm Sheriff Riley, and I'll be leading this case." Riley's words started to break up as he tried to sound like he was in control. However, this was his first *real* case outside of speeding tickets and jaywalking and he was scared to death.

He cleared his throat. "What do we have here, officer?" he said to the much older, seasoned officer.

The officer smiled at Riley. "The first case, huh?" He patted Riley on the back like they had been compadres for years. "Well, don't you worry. You'll do just fine. We all had to start somewhere, right?"

He patted Riley on the back again and then cleared his throat as a look of disgust and anguish washed over his face.

"For starters, I've never seen anything like this. In all my years, I don't recall anything ever like this happening here," the plump man said wiping his brow. "And as crazy as all of this looks, in the end it's pretty darn simple."

"What do you mean?" asked Riley.

"I don't know why they even called you boys in. The groundskeeper, JD, did it. He left a note and everything," the officer said in a matter-of-fact tone while passing Riley a piece of paper.

Riley opened the rain-soaked note and read:

They shouldn't have done this to me.
My house needs me.
I had to stop them.
They had to die.

Riley had a puzzled look on his face as he tucked the now contaminated note into an evidence bag and zipped it.

"This still doesn't explain what happened or why he killed himself. Who'd you say this guy was? The note sounds more of what a maniac would write."

The officer just shook his head. "Hmm, maybe that's where you come in. Let's get out of the rain. Come along, I'll show you the crime scene and tell you what we know. Maybe you will understand how much of a maniac groundskeeper we're dealing with."

As Riley walked through the front door, a cold chill running over him, he pulled his light rain jacket closer around him. The house was as magnificent as he had always imagined it to be. Standing in the foyer, you could get the layout of the whole house. The winding staircase lay directly in front of them, running wild towards the upper rooms. To his left was the sitting room with deep dark cherry wood panels across the wall. The furniture seemed almost too elegant to touch with the burgundy and gold trim and plastic still covering each cushion. Not a speck of dust was anywhere to be seen, but still, the smell wasn't right. The air was old and stale, musky if you will, not an aroma you would imagine when looking upon such elegance. Off towards the rear of the sitting room, you could see the kitchen area as it wrapped around the length of the back of the house. To the right was the living room. It seemed detached from the foyer, not as open as the sitting room. *Must be for privacy from the outside world,* he thought.

It was so cold in the house that he could see the officer's breath like smoke coming from a cigarette as he spoke, just as if they were standing outside on a cold winter's morning.

"Why is it so cold in here? It's the middle of fall."

"They're saying the radiator must be broken or something. There is no other explanation for a cold like this. You could almost hang meat in here." The officer shivered, knowing how ridiculous it sounded. "Maybe that was a poor analogy," he said as he led Riley into the other room.

"Over here in the living room is where we found Mrs. Setliff. She received four hard blows to the back of the head. We're pretty sure she never saw it coming. It's a real shame. The neighbors say she was a fine old lady, not a care in the world. She was a good, honest, church-going lady who was always ready to lend a hand around the community."

"Odd, I heard that no one liked her and her husband. The way the town whispers about it, this was more of an expected thing. No one seems shocked at all," Riley said, confused.

"Her husband? No. He was a peculiar one. He was fine up until a few years back, matter of fact about the time they started construction on Willow's Dawn. But her? She was the most loved lady in town, well up to about three weeks ago. We're not quite clear on what happened up here. The family kept it pretty hush, hush. We heard it had something to do with their granddaughter, Jennifer. She's seven. We're trying to get a hold of Social

Services to get it cleared up," the officer summarized. "Frankly, though, I don't think they're connected, so I wouldn't even waste your time. She hasn't been here since that day."

Riley wondered what made the officer so convinced that the two were not related. He said up until three weeks ago that everyone loved Mrs. Setliff. He also said three weeks ago that something happened with her granddaughter, which got Social Services involved. What happened to make this town rally against this beautiful, church-going pillar of the community? Something had to be there, why the sudden change in behavior? He took it all down in his notebook.

The living room was well organized and neatly kept. Under the far window was a soft, beige davenport with a small, dragon-clawed, cherry table next to it with a beautiful arrangement of flowers on top. Family pictures lined the blood-splattered walls and mantle. Across the living room was a doorway that led into the kitchen. You could barely make it out through the strong stench of decay, but there was a sweet aroma of an apple pie cooling on the stovetop.

Riley looked at the bloodstain on the rug and the blood splatter on the walls and ceiling. *Such force and anger were used. This seemed more like blind rage than murder.* "Looking at the widespread pattern, I would say the culprit was a fairly decent sized man, young and able to pack quite a punch. Have you recovered the murder weapon?" Riley asked.

The officer pointed to a large metal pipe across the room. "We think he must have used that, but there is no blood on it. We're not sure if we should take it into evidence or not." Riley looked over at the large piece of metal. He walked across the room to examine it closer.

Admittedly, we are missing something. How could this be the weapon used? But how could it not be the weapon used? The blood splatter alone was enough to pinpoint it to an object such as this, but why clean it if you're just going to kill yourself anyway? What are we missing? Riley thought as he scribbled erratically in his notebook.

The older officer continued, interrupting Riley's thoughts and bringing him back to the crime scene.

"And another thing, the groundskeeper happened to be an old man, matter of fact, older than me. He was a short, skinny, frail, little man, so no theory there, aye?" The officer wrinkled his nose and let out a puzzled sigh. "Well, if you're ready? It's the same scenario with Mr. Setliff. Here, I'll show you."

With that, the officer walked out of the living room and started up the winding staircase.

"Mr. Setliff was here in his office," he said, opening the door.

The office was dark and messy, not at all like the living room. Papers and bank statements were thrown around all over the furniture and floor. A very untidy bookcase lined the far wall and you could still smell the smoke from a cigar lingering in the air, as if it were sitting lit on the desk right in front of you.

"He was sitting at his desk over there," pointing into a dark corner. "As like Mrs. Setliff, he also received blows to the back of the head, how many we're not sure. They were at such a force that that I'm sure Mr. Setliff will be deemed unrecognizable. Very brutal. It is the most horrible image I have ever had to witness."

The officer flipped the desktop light on, and light filled up the room. Riley grabbed his handkerchief and brought it to his mouth as nausea rushed over him.

"I'm sorry, I forgot to mention we're still waiting for the other coroner's vehicle. We can't touch the body until he's seen it."

There on the floor behind the desk was Mr. Setliff. He had fallen forward due to the blows and crumpled on the floor next to his overturned chair. It was hard to make out any details about him. He was in all sense of the word, gone. His clothing was covered in blood, more blood than you would think could come from any one human, beaten with such force that you could barely make out the even the structure of a skull.

"Officer, can we say for a fact that this is, I mean was, Mr. Setliff? Is there anyone who can identify him?" Riley could hear the officer talking, but he wasn't listening. His question was nothing more than a stalling mechanism, a way for him to find his next words. It was apparent to all involved who this man was lying on the floor in a broken heap of bone and matter. *Such force, so much hatred and rage, there has to be more to this story.*

Riley gasped, trying hard to stay in control of the situation. The smell was unbearable. It wasn't the smell of death – it was more. The odor reminded him of the roadkill that laid baked in the hot afternoon sun. *They must have been dead for days.* "How long has it been since they found the bodies? What can you tell me about the murder weapon?"

"Same problem as with the Missus." The officer pointed to a clean, blunt object next to the body. "Someone broke off the handle from the other chair, but once again, it has no blood. I don't know what to make of all of this. The coroner placed Mrs. Setliff's death at no more than three hours ago."

"Three hours ago?" Riley asked in disbelief. *That's unreal,* he thought. *The smell, it shouldn't be so strong, especially with the house being so cold. What are we missing?* "What about Mr. Setliff? Tell me what he was like," Riley said while feverishly jotting down notes and trying to keep his nose covered from the horrendous smell.

"He was much different from Mrs. Setliff. He didn't go to church, even on the holidays. He didn't get out much since retiring from his building profession. He'd pretty much kept himself busy here finishing Willow's Dawn. Not too many people could stand him, a real peculiar fellow, stubborn and rude," the officer described. "No one understood how Mrs. Setliff actually stayed with him for so many years. I guess opposites do attract."

Riley tried to take everything in, but none of it was making sense. "So, the note says the groundskeeper did it. What was the motive?"

"They spoke to one of the Setliff's friends down the road and she says they were going to fire JD, something about his obsession with the house and their granddaughter, Jennifer. They felt like they were in danger," explained the officer.

"I thought you said the granddaughter had nothing to do with this. Now you say the man who killed the Setliff's was obsessed with their granddaughter?" Riley took a long pause, but the officer did not explain.

"Still, why would he kill himself? Suicide doesn't make any sense. Where did he kill himself?" Riley said abruptly, feeling like he was getting somewhere, but he wasn't sure where.

"He hung himself in the cellar. Isn't that where all the deranged lunatics kill themselves?" the officer said with a laugh. When he saw Riley was not amused, he stopped short.

"Ahem, the cellar is off the kitchen. Let's go."

The officer scratched his head. "You know, before you showed up alone, we really thought you'd have that physic lady with you."

Riley raised an eyebrow. "Physic lady?"

"Yeah, that Madam Zola lady you state boys like to use for those weird, supernatural problems."

"I would hardly call kidnappings and missing persons supernatural problems," Riley said rolling his eyes.

"Well you have to admit, this isn't your normal murder/suicide here."

As the two gentlemen walked down the staircase, Riley couldn't help but stop and notice some of the family pictures. On the wall leading down the stairs was an entourage of photographs dating from the Setliff's wedding. Each image depicted an ever-loving environment, the birth of children, more marriages, the births of what was probably grandchildren and great-grandchildren. There seemed to be a reoccurring factor in most of the pictures: a small, frail-looking man. It would appear he was part of the family. *Could this be the groundskeeper?* Riley thought.

The officer noticed Riley looking at the picture. "That's JD, the groundskeeper. Doesn't paint much of a picture of a killer, does he?"

"He doesn't, but I don't think we need Madam Zola to tell us who did" Riley said finishing the decent down the stairs.

When the officer opened the cellar door, a rush of arctic-like air came up from the depths.

"Watch your step, Sheriff. One of my officers fell earlier today. I believe it's cold enough to form ice on 'em," he pointed at the steps as he descended the stairs.

You could smell the blood and the rot from the top of the stairs. It became stronger with every step. Riley grabbed his handkerchief to control his stomach again. In the middle of the stairwell was the string for the light. Before the officer pulled it, he turned to Riley and said, "Prepare yourself. The coroner hasn't released the body yet."

The light swayed back and forth, lighting up each part of the cellar one by one. Riley watched for a moment the body leaving and coming into view with the swinging of the light bulb. It was the small, frail-looking, old man from the pictures. Not the killer that could have mutilated this couple so violently. *How did he muster up the strength to do such a thing? He was a quarter size of Mr. Setliff.* None of this was making any sense. As Riley watched, he noticed something on the wall.

"Is there something written on that far wall? Stop the light. I can't see anything with it swaying like that," Riley ordered.

The officer grabbed the string to tame it. "Yes, there is. I think it was to throw us off. I don't know, it just doesn't make any sense."

Riley grunted, "Does any of this make any sense?"

On the far wall, it was written in the same script as the note.

HELP ME

***

Present

The rain was pounding hard on the windows when I awoke from my catatonic slumber. Where am I? As my eyes started to focus on the darkness, I could see that I wasn't in my bedroom anymore. I sat up with a jerk, feeling a searing pain in my leg as I slowly remembered what was happening. There was a man in my house, and he was trying to kill me.

CHAPTER ONE

Three Months Ago

I gasped as I looked through the windshield at the most magnificent house I had ever seen. She never ceased to amaze me, as the feelings and the shivers were almost too much to handle. There, up high on the edge of the cliff, surrounded by an army of willow trees, she stood Willow's Dawn. I pulled my clunking, old, blue Ford Fairlane up the cobblestone driveway and got out. Wow, I hadn't seen anything quite like her in a very long time, and now she was all mine.

The air coming off of the ocean was crisp, as it usually was this time of year, so I reached back into my car and pulled out my turquoise sweater since the cold air got the best of me. I could smell the salt in the air, and it reminded me of a simpler time back when I was young and full of life. Willow's Dawn always gave me such a sense of peace and happiness. I looked towards the house again and began to get all giddy inside. This was mine. All *mine*. I flung my arms out and started twirling around, laughing and soaking up the refreshing ocean air just like I used to do when I was a little girl.

She was beautiful, almost as beautiful as I remembered. The paint was starting to peel in many spots, but she still had a look of sheer elegance. The Victorian four-story plantation had four columns along the front and a porch that wrapped around to the back to the veranda. The front door was protected by an archway made up of a flourishing rose vine. It was almost as if someone had put it there to keep something out. You could see that the roof was badly in need of repair, *but with a little love and a lot of work, she will be home again,* I thought with a smile.

The azalea bushes that lined the driveway up to the front of the house were blooming white and pink shaggy flowers. In reality, I couldn't believe they were still alive. All they needed was a proper pruning and they would look as brilliant as my mind could see. It was clear that someone was taking care of Willow's Dawn, and whomever they left in charge loved her as much as my grandparents did.

I followed the broken, cobblestone path around to the back of the house and stood at the edge of the cliff. As I looked down at the rocks below, a sense of panic washed over me while the ocean waves crashed upon them. The sound was almost deafening, like thunder clapping all around me. A cold chill ran down my spine as the ocean air whipped through my hair. I felt a force forming all around my body as I began feeling lightheaded and dizzy, like I was going to fall. I backed up quickly and turned to run away from this incredible feeling of danger and uneasiness. As I turned to flee, I ran into a little, old man. He had dark, troublesome eyes that seemed to pierce my very soul. I screamed as I turned to run in the other direction, but once again, I was back at the edge of the cliff. I had nowhere to hide.

I turned to face the old man again and screamed over the roaring waves, "Who are you?" as I brushed the hair out of my face in a nervous manner. I looked the man over and realized he probably couldn't hurt me anyway. He was all of five feet two inches with a little bit of a hunch in his back and worn, tattered clothes covering his body. He looked quite frail and harmless, but then again, so did Ted Bundy.

"My name is Joseph. I am the groundskeeper here at Willow's Dawn. I have been expecting you, Miss. Jennifer," the old man replied in a strong, southern accent. His breath was hot and reeked of something dead. "I have come to show you the house. I hope you don't mind," he said, extending his arm for me to take hold. I looked at the old man, confused and even a little shocked as I refused.

Yes, I minded. He just scared the crap out of me, how was I not going to mind? I smiled as best I could and said, "Thank you, Joseph, but that won't be necessary. I grew up here and can find my way around just fine." I tried not to sound rude, but by the look on his face, I had not succeeded.

Joseph narrowed his eyes and looked at me. "You say you grew up here? Ma'am, please forgive me, but I have been this here's groundskeeper for many years, and never did a child ever live here," he said accusingly.

"I didn't live here. However, this was a place I visited quite often -- often enough to know my way around," I said, smiling. What I said was a lie. I didn't remember anything about this house, not even why I was not allowed to come back or how my grandparents died. Everything about this house was a glob in the back of my mind. But I wasn't going to tell him that.

"Excuse me, Ma'am, but am I making you nervous? You seem a little jittery, on edge, so to speak," he said with a laugh as he looked at the edge of the cliff under my feet. "Why don't we go inside, and I'll make us a nice, hot cup of tea. Wouldn't that be something nice," Joseph said, turning towards the house, pulling at the air as if to coax me along.

He was a strange, little man. Joseph acted as if he didn't know me, but then had said he had been expecting me. When I looked closer at him, it seemed like I knew him from somewhere, but couldn't tell you how or where from. And yet, I knew I had never seen him before in my life.

At this point, I knew the only way to get rid of him would be to tolerate him. So, I walked towards the house for a "nice, hot cup of tea."

As we walked across the yard, the wind let out a scream of anguish and the trees swayed in the wind. The leaves rustled together in such a way it was almost like they were whispering and calling out my name. I stopped and tried to listen again, to make out what it was that I was hearing, but Joseph called from the doorway.

"Ma'am, don't you be listening to the trees. They get all gossipy when new people come around, always trying to start trouble."

I thought it was odd that he seemed to know what I was doing, and what sounded like a joke instead left me feeling uneasy and unsure of what to make of my current situation. As I approached the back door, I heard Joseph cry out.

"No! Don't!"

I looked at Joseph and asked, "Don't what?"

He looked at me, puzzled for a moment, then rushed over to me and looked out the back door. "Uh…. don't... fall. These brick steps are mighty old. Don't want you hurting yourself," he said with a small, half laugh.

He looked out toward the willow trees again and then shut the door.

It was much colder inside the old house than it was outside, which struck me as odd being that the weather was just starting to change. Usually, the homes are still sweltering and humid inside, leaving its residents sitting outside on the porch in the fresh air with a glass of iced tea for relief. I shivered again as I pulled my sweater tighter around me and glanced around the kitchen.

"Ma'am, are you cold?" Joseph asked puzzled and as I nodded, he said, "It's not cold in here, Missy. It's as hot as a firecracker on the Fourth of July."

Now granted, it wasn't mid-December, but it certainly wasn't mid-July. I didn't know what this man's game was, but he was really starting to frighten me.

"Joseph? Did you say you were expecting me? How did you know I was coming?" I asked, with my hands slightly shaking from the bitter cold.

Joseph looked at me for a minute, like he was trying to weigh out all of his options.

"Well, the real estate office called me this morning, said you were coming to the house today and to make sure the house was ready for you," he said, nodding and smiling brightly.

I tried to think back to when I called the office and what I had told them, but I couldn't recall anything. I just shrugged it off. What reason would this man have to lie to me? How else would he have known if this wasn't true? I smiled at him as I lifted my cup for another drink.

***

After Joseph left, I wandered around the old house. I still couldn't believe that I was finally back wandering these old halls, and the thought of her being all mine made me swell inside. Life couldn't be better, and I couldn't be happier.

After my grandparents passed away, the house went through various owners, but they all ended up leaving after short periods. It wasn't clear why they left. The real estate office called and said they couldn't keep it on the market any longer, and the only right thing to do was to give it back to the original owners. The bank agreed, so now she was mine. I smiled at the thought. No one loved her as much as our family did. When the bank called, I immediately decided I would move in and take on the responsibility of looking after her. I had nothing to lose. I was just hoping to find out more about my family. Why so many secrets? Why did my grandparents mysteriously die? Why was I not allowed to come here ever again when I was so happy here? Anything and everything, I just wanted to know, and being here at Willow's Dawn was just the place to start.

***

"Chief, I think we have a problem," the young rookie detective said, busting through the door of Chief Detective Riley's office.

"What the hell are you doing, boy? Where's the fire?" Riley yelled at Officer Nichols.

Nichols was assigned to Riley a little over six months ago. It was supposed to be a simple "take the boy and turn him into a man" assignment. Someone to be proud of, someone as good as Riley. It was a rocky start for the first few weeks, but then the kid started to grow on him, and it was no secret that Riley could use someone to talk to and help out with cases.

"This better be good. I'm starting my vacation in fifteen minutes." The older officer said as he looked at his wrist and his imaginary watch.

Nichols looked at Riley not sure if he should continue. His partner could be fickle. You never really knew when he would blow up or when he would agree with you. His job had been hard on him over the years, something you could see in every line on his face. "It's about that old house, the one on the cliff, the one you seem so bewitched by."

In the few, short months that Nichols had worked side by side with Riley, he got to learn more about the old house on the cliff called Willow's Dawn. He had become as fascinated with it as Riley was, but would never tell him that. When he was little, he had heard stories about the place. Some say it's haunted. Some say they have witnessed ghosts walking the grounds on stormy nights. It's funny how once you become an adult, the stories just seem to disappear. Well, except for him. He asked Riley one night if he had ever heard any of the campfire stories about the old place. Riley just waved his hand and told him *"it was nonsense" and he wasn't "going to fall into all that supernatural mumbo jumbo."* He had asked Riley why he called in the old physic Madam Zola for special cases if he didn't believe in her abilities. *All Riley said was that she knows things.* Nichols said, "Yeah, supernatural mumbo jumbo." Riley was all fact and no fiction, as strait-laced as they came. He was a stand-up, by-the-book cop, and the whole town knew it. It was an honor to be trained by the best detective in town, and knowing he was the lead Sheriff on that notorious night made it all that much sweeter.

Coming back to the present, Nichols saw Riley's feet fell off his desk as he sat straight up. "Go on, boy, tell me."

Riley knew this was the break he had been waiting for. He had been trying to bust this case for almost twenty years now, and the look in this boy's eyes was like gold to him.

Nichols took a deep breath. "Someone has moved in up there."

Riley sighed, leaned back, and propped his feet back up on the desk. "This is news? This is the fire?" He was very annoyed with this boy. Every little thing caused him to panic or overreact. "There have been thirty or more people move in and out of there over the years. I can't waste my time with this. I have to get home and pack, plus my dog's waiting on her dinner," Riley said with an annoyed tone.

With that, Riley stood up and made his way to the door, but Nichols stood and blocked his way, calmly stating, "It's the granddaughter."

Riley took a step back and thought he was going to fall, so he grabbed the door frame to steady himself. Riley's face went white. "You're joking, right?" He didn't wait for an answer, as he just pushed Nichols aside and ran out of the police station's door. Nichols turned and started running right behind him.

***

It amazed me how every previous owner tried to preserve our family. Our pictures were still lining the mantle and hung on the walls. *It was almost as if my grandparents had never left this old place*, I thought as I made my way up the attic stairs to search out my past.

The heavy door creaked loudly above my head as it slowly opened. The dust filled my lungs and I started to cough like I had been smoking for thirty years. When I finished pulling myself up through the door, I looked for something to prop it open and help circulate some fresh air in. I leaned over to grab a long box and a moving shadow caught the corner of my eye. I jumped and the attic door fell out of my hand with a loud, dusty **thump**. "Crap, now what?" I said aloud. I knew I could get it back open, but it wouldn't be an easy task since the handle looked to be broken on this side of the door. "Hello? Is there someone there?" I looked around the ever-dimming, hazy room and wondered where I had put my flashlight. There was only one window up here, and with the storm clouds moving in, the light was fading fast.

I heard a shuffling noise from the opposite corner of the attic, and I slowly walked over to see what it was. It was coming from a piece of old furniture that was covered with a dust cloth. The cloth was barely moving when I leaned in closer to grab the bottom of it and reveal its contents underneath. There was something under there. I was too afraid to move. I didn't know what to do. I wasn't as brave as I had thought.

All of a sudden, the sheet catapulted off of the couch and flew towards me as I let out a horrified scream.

***

As Riley and Nichols got out of the car, they heard the shrill sound of a girl screaming. It was Riley's worst fear: it was happening again. They rushed to the door and began knocking rapidly. When no one answered, they loudly announced their presence and that they were coming in, then broke in the door.

The screaming had stopped by the time they had entered the house, and all was quiet. The last time Riley had been in Willow's Dawn was the night of the murders. The same horrid feeling he had had that night was now back again, and that smell. He could swear he still smelt it, week-old, rotting flesh that had only been dead for three mere hours. He knew there was something wrong but never figured out what.

"You check the downstairs, I'm going up. If you find anything at all, just yell and I'll come running," Riley said to Nichols. Nichols nodded and held his gun out for protection.

Nichols had never been in the house before, but everything he had ever been told and every childhood urban legend came rushing back all at once. Even though he was a grown man, he still felt like that scared, little kid. Nick tried to laugh at himself but couldn't even muster the strength. As he walked around the corner into the living room, he felt the hair on the back of his neck rise up in defense. It was if his body had felt it coming at that moment. He heard the first real clap of thunder, and everything went dark.

"Riley!" Nichols yelled, but Riley didn't respond. "Damned transformer," he cursed.

Nichols went for his flashlight, but his fingers could do nothing more than fumble their way around his belt. He continued to make his way along the wall, holding on to it and following it like a never-ending maze. Everything he touched felt wet and sticky. Like the flip of a switch, the smell hit his nostrils, burning all the way up and taking his breath away. He couldn't quite put his finger on it. It was as if someone had filled the entire room with rotting roadkill. It was overpowering and sickening.

Nichols had never been more scared in his life. He began screaming Riley's name over and over again as he sobbed. *Something was wrong. Why won't Riley answer me?* Something ran across his feet and made him trip. As he scrambled forward onto his knees, he pushed himself into a corner until he felt secure enough to stand back up. He couldn't move, as he felt someone in there with him. "Riley?" he cried looking through the darkness. Finally, Nichols saw a tinge of light coming from in front of him. With a sigh of relief, he scurried forward.

The closer he traveled to the light source, the stronger the smell became, and the louder the storm raged. He knew Riley would never be able to hear him over the wind, so he just concentrated on trying to find his way out and to the safety of the police car outside.

The light source appeared to be the moonlight peering in through the back door window. Nichols ran to the door and tried to open it, but it wouldn't budge. He fumbled with the locks and finally released it and tried the door again. It still wouldn't open. Nichols began banging on the door, screaming and crying as loud as he could, hoping that Riley would hear him. The stories, all the stories from when he was a kid, flashed like lightning through his head. He knew he was about to die. He looked down at his hands and they were all wet and sticky covered in a thick red substance. *Blood*, he thought, that's what the wet sticky substance must have been on the walls. He glanced back towards the other room. It was all happening again. The high-pitched squeal of a rusty door began to slowly open. The noise was coming from behind him. He couldn't move. Nichols's heart stopped as he slowly turned towards the noise. The cellar door was opening. Nichols slid to the floor as the figure of a man became clearer. All he could do was cry and holding his face in his hands.

***

Riley made his way up the stairs with his gun held out in front of him. There were historical pictures hung on the wall of the winding staircase. That night came back to him so vividly, it was like the pictures had never moved. Surely the other residents would have taken down the Setliff's pictures? He stopped for a moment and stared at a picture of Eleanor Setliff. How regal and elegant she was, though he had only seen her once, and that was the night of the murder. He had to fight his mind to get those pictures out of his head.

He stopped when he saw something run past the top railing but couldn't make out what it had been. Then he heard another scream. He didn't think, he just ran towards the voice.

At the end of the stairwell was a long hallway and, in the middle, he could see the attic stairs were down, but the door shut. He wasn't sure which way to go at this point until he heard the girl's voice again.

"Let me out, you stupid door!"

Riley was thrown back by the lack of fear coming from the tone, which was slightly amusing as he pieced together the night's events in his mind. He made his way up the attic stairs.

"Ma'am?" he yelled out.

"Who is that?" I yelled back.

"I'm Detective Riley. I work down at the police station. My partner and I came to investigate and heard you screaming. Is everything all right?"

"Well, it would be if you'd lift this stupid door. It's stuck, and I can't get out," I said rudely, banging on it some more. *Who the heck was this guy? Was he just going to leave me stuck up here all night?*

Riley laughed to himself as he pushed open the door to uncover the most beautiful face he had ever seen. "Ma'am," Riley smiled, tipping his hat.

I smiled back and nodded my head in acknowledgment. "Detective," I said. After a few moments of no other movement, I raised an eyebrow as I pushed past him down the attic stairs.

***

Nichols finally stopped sobbing long enough to get up the courage and look again towards the cellar door. Slowly, he raised his head. The first thing he noticed was the lack of blood that was once on his hands. The lights flickered back on, and Nichols jumped to his feet. The cellar door was still closed, and there was no blood and no smell. He didn't know what was going on. It was like everything he just witnessed had all disappeared. He swung the kitchen back door open as fast as he could and ran out of the house to wait for Riley in the squad car.

CHAPTER TWO

"So detective, what brings you up here to my hill? Did I scream that loud?" I asked, making my way to the kitchen downstairs. "Can I make you a cup of tea or coffee?"

I stepped onto the stairs and it creaked under me. I jumped and gasped, then looked at the detective, hoping he didn't notice.

"Yes, that would be great. My partner is down there somewhere, securing the place," he said with a half-hearted laugh.

Lifting an eyebrow, I asked, "Why would I need securing, Detective?"

"We heard you scream and thought you were in danger. That's why we came in to look around," Riley said proudly. "We'll be fixing your door. I'm really sorry about that."

"My door?" I said, rushing down the rest of the stairs. I sighed as I looked at the object in question.

"We'll fix what we can tonight to keep you safe and then get it replaced for you in the morning," he said, embarrassed.

I laughed as I thought of the situation upstairs. "I guess it serves me right," I said with a smile. *He was definitely too cute to be mad at.* "I was upstairs looking around and I was hoping to find something that would help me understand my family better, and well," I almost couldn't contain my laughter by then and giggled out, "I saw a sheet move. I freaked out. It was the biggest rat I have ever seen, had to be at least two feet." I held my hands about 3 feet apart in astonishment.

Riley snickered. "Two feet, huh? I'm not sure if I've ever seen a rat that big."

"Okay, well, maybe not two feet," I blushed, "but it was the biggest I have ever seen." We both had a good laugh over my findings on the way to the kitchen.

"Hey Nichols, stand down. It was only a killer rat," Riley said with a laugh.

Riley received nothing but silence as a response. "Nichols?" Riley said, looking puzzled. "Well, where did he go?"

"Maybe the rat got him," I said, laughing. Riley turned my way to acknowledge my words but didn't smile at my morbid sense of humor. He looked uneasy and concerned. Still, I just shrugged it off to my imagination. My scare upstairs must really had rattled my nerves and I needed to relax.

Riley pulled his gun out from his belt, raised his arm, and pulled me behind him. *What in the world was going on? This is my house*, I thought as he turned towards me and placed his finger to his lips to quiet me. There was a bumping noise coming from the kitchen.

"Nichols? Are you there?" the detective spoke as he tried not to sound alarmed, but I could hear the uncertainty in his voice.

BAM!

I screamed and dropped the flashlight after hearing the loud noise coming from the kitchen area. "Was that him?" I said, shakily.

"I don't know, but stay close behind me," he said, bravely.

"They really messed up with the insulation in this house. It's freezing in here," I offered, trying to keep the conversation light.

Riley remembered that horrid night and how cold the house felt. "Yeah, it's always been like that."

I was thrown back by what he had said. "What do you mean '*always*?' What's going on, and what are you doing here?" I said. With that, the police cruiser's horn blew frantically. Riley ran into the kitchen. The back door was banging in the wind.

"Miss, I'd better go. It sounds like we may have a possible call. The bang must have been Nichols running out the door, no need to be alarmed. It was a pleasure meeting you and if you need anything, please don't hesitate to call." Riley said, ignoring my questions and handing me his card.

"But what did you mean?" I yelled after him, but I was too late, as he rushed out of the kitchen door.

"Great," I thought, "what a nice welcoming group they have here."

***

As Nichols sat in the cruiser waiting for Riley, he thought about everything that had happened in the kitchen: the blood, the cellar door, and especially the image at the top of the cellar stairs. All of it was horrifying. Everything that he knew about the house was right. He couldn't tell Riley though, as he would never believe him. Riley was too much of a skeptic and would just chalk it up to his childhood phobias. Nick hoped Riley and the girl were all right, but he had to get out of that house. Nick peered out the window toward the house, scanning the windows of the house for movement but saw nothing. Then, as he noticed a shadow out of the corner of his eye.

He slowly turned his head and peered through the attic window. It looked like a man was standing there staring at the car, but it wasn't Riley. Nichols panicked and laid into the cruiser's horn to get Riley's attention. They had to get out of there. Now!

***

Riley jumped into the cruiser next to Nichols. "What is it?"

"We have to go! Now!" Nichols screamed abruptly. His hands were shaking as he sat behind the wheel. "We need to get back to headquarters," he lied.

"Okay, but maybe I should drive. You don't look so good."

"I'm fine. Let's just go." By this point, Nichols was almost whimpering. All he wanted to do was get out of there. Whatever evil was residing in that house, it was far more potent than this police duo could handle.

***

I sat down at the kitchen table with my cup of tea and thought about the strange encounter with Detective Riley. *What brought him out here in the first place? What did they want? Did he know something that would help me with my past? Could he help me find out why I never returned to Willow's Dawn?* All these questions swirled inside my head as my eyes began to focus on the cellar door, zeroing in on the unlatched deadbolt.

I slowly stood up from the table as I moved closer to the cellar. In the short time that I had been here, I had never had any reason to venture down there and had kept the door bolted shut. A shiver ran down my spine as I reached for the knob. It was ice cold. I jumped back a bit, taken off guard. I quickly bolted the door and turned to make sure the back door was also bolted. *Nichols must have gone down there while he was here*, I thought to myself.

The storm outside started up again, and I could feel the thunder rip through the house as the lights began flickering. I rolled my eyes in frustration as I turned on some music, gathered up all of the candles I could find, and headed upstairs towards my refuge – the bath.

Having reached the bathroom, I set up the candles around the dragon-claw, antique tub and drew a hot bath full of soapy bubbles. I slowly escaped down into the water and quietly drifted off to sleep to the low hum of the music coming from the parlor downstairs.

I was a little girl again, so happy and full of life. My grandparents were sitting on the veranda, watching me chase the butterflies and, like a broken record, cautioning me to be careful and look out for the cliff's edge. Everyone was happy, but something was wrong. I couldn't think straight. I was there whirling around and around in circles, and they were laughing at me. I was going faster and faster, giggling uncontrollably. I could barely recognize their faces, blurry as they were, and then their faces changed entirely. Their laughter morphed into what sounded like a multitude of banshees, demonic and evil. I stopped laughing and became scared. Then, I saw him. I tried to stop spinning, but I fell to the ground, all dizzy and nauseous. When I looked up, I saw a tall, old man in front of me. He looked like someone I knew, but I couldn't put my finger on it. I was scared and yelled for my grandma, but she was still laughing at me. Everything was spinning out of control when the old man's face changed, where had I seen him before. I tried to flee, but he grabbed hold of me as I kicked and swung my arms, crying for help.

I woke up abruptly, flinging my arms and splashing water all over the bathroom tile. My heart raced when I realized the power had gone out while I was resting, and now with all my flailing, my floor was half-flooded with water. I had lost all but two of my candles. I looked around the bathroom, waiting for my eyes to adjust as an unsettling feeling entered my stomach. Something was wrong. A moment later, I heard a loud bang coming from downstairs and jumped out of the bath, grabbing my bathrobe and the flashlight from under the sink as I cautiously headed down the long stairwell.

Just my luck, halfway down the staircase, my batteries started getting weak. "I must be in a movie. This isn't happening," I said, rolling my eyes. As my flashlight flickered off and on, it created a strobe-light effect with the occasional, eerie flash of lightning coming in unsteady.

I made my way along the wall towards the kitchen. I was terrified. Something wasn't right. Something was very wrong.

"Hello?" I cried out. I sensed a presence, but I knew I was alone. *I'd seen it in the movies a thousand times, the dumb blonde always dies first*, I couldn't even laugh at the thought. I could feel the coldness along with a breeze the closer I got to the kitchen. Why would I feel a breeze? There was just enough moonlight to brighten the kitchen area, so I turned off my disco strobe and looked around the corner. I let out a small giggle when I saw the back door flying in the wind. I laughed at myself as I ran to shut it. The storm had blown it open. I couldn't believe I was such a baby. I turned my back to the door and giggled as my eyes caught sight of the unlatched deadbolt of the cellar door.

I felt my heart stop. I knew I had locked both doors. What was going on? This time, I grabbed the doorknob and slowly opened the cellar door. The cold, stale air knocked me back as I tried to stay calm. "Hello? Is there anyone there?" I didn't want an answer to that question, but I didn't know what else to do. There was an awful stench coming from below, and I had to turn my head to gasp for a breath of fresher air. I walked to the first step and tried to find the string for the light, then I heard a creak from a lower plank. My heart raced with fear. I turned around and ran back into the kitchen, slamming and locking the cellar door as I fell to the floor crying. *What was happening?* I grabbed my cell phone and the card from the counter.

***

It was 3 a.m. when Riley's phone rang. He rolled over and fumbled for the light, knocking it off the table. "Crap," he mumbled as he found the phone. "Riley here. This had better be important."

"Detective Riley? It's me, Jenny Murphy," I said sobbing. "You told me to call you if I had a problem. Someone's in my house."

"I'll be there in a minute," Riley stuttered, hanging up the phone. As he sat on the side of the bed pulling on his boots, his emotions raged as that horrid night came flooding back. Whatever had happened all of those years ago was possibly happening again.

CHAPTER THREE

I tried to calm my nerves with a hot cup of tea as I waited for Detective Riley to show up. I sat at the kitchen table with my eyes fixed on the cellar deadbolt. I wasn't going to take any chances this time. My hands were shaking as I reached for my cup to take a drink just as someone pounded on the back door. I felt the hot tea pierce my skin as I jumped up from the table. "Ow," I winced as I went for the door. "Detective, I'm so glad to see…" My voice trailed off as I looked at the little, old man from earlier standing in the rain. "Oh, I'm sorry. I was expecting someone else."

"A detective?" asked Joseph. "Is something amiss, ma'am? You need some help?"

"No, no, Joseph. May I ask what you're doing here this late at night?" There was something about this little man that I didn't like. Maybe it was the way his beady, little, black eyes looked straight through me, even when he was talking to me. Perhaps it was the way his voice seemed to growl, raspy and monotone with no feeling in any of his words. There was still a strange feeling of recognition, but I wasn't sure from where. This nagging feeling wouldn't let me be. I felt that I knew him, but, how could I? I had only seen him for the first time a few weeks ago. I remembered someone vaguely from my summers here at Willow's Dawn, a man who took care of my grandparents and their home. I couldn't remember his name, but *why* couldn't I remember his name? The one thing I was sure of was that this man scared the hell out of me, and I just wanted him to go away.

He pushed his way passed me in the doorway as he muttered, "Maybe we should take you to go have a lie-down, huh Missy? Wouldn't that be something nice?"

I just looked at him not knowing what to say. If I flat out told him to leave, would he be crazy enough to freak out on me? I was hoping Riley would get here and tell this man to leave me alone, but I didn't know when he would get here. I just had to bite the bullet and hope. "Joseph, I know you want to help, and I know you care about me and this house," I said in the kindest way possible, "but it's late. I don't think you should be here right now, and anyway the detective will be here soon, so you needn't worry about me. Why did you say you were here again?" I said, puzzled.

Joseph's eyes darkened, and he lowered his voice as he whispered, "You don't trust old Joseph now, do ya, Missy?" He looked down and continued, "I sensed you were in trouble, so I came to check up on ya. That is all it is ma'am, so nothing to worry you. Now let's go upstairs and I'll put ya to bed. You'll feel better in the morn." He said as he reached for my elbow.

"Don't touch me," I said, jerking my arm away, "and get out of my house." I was sure he could see the terror in my eyes as I slowly backed away from him.

"Now ma'am, don't ya go being like that. I've been the groundskeeper for years before you got here, and I'm gonna keep on being the keeper, even if I have to take care of you now," he said slowly walking towards me.

"No, leave me alone! Go away. I don't need you to take care of me." I turned around, ran through the living room to the front door, opened the door, and cried, "Just leave me alone!" I screamed as I ran right into Detective Riley.

"Whoa, whoa, whoa. You called me, remember?" He stood there as I collapsed into his arms out of fear.

"Make him go away. Make him leave me alone." I wept hysterically.

"Who? What happened? Are you okay? Did they hurt you?" There were so many questions, yet all I could do was point towards the kitchen's entryway.

Riley slowly walked into the living room. The lights flickered back on, and I let out a sigh of relief.

"It's the groundskeeper, Joseph. I met him the other day when I was moving in. He's weird and scary, and he's in the kitchen," I said with my voice still shaking.

Riley walked into the empty kitchen and looked around. "Well, there's no one here now."

"He was here. He was trying to get me upstairs to lie down, said he would take care of me. I was so scared. There's something strange about him, but I can't explain it. I want you to find him and tell him to leave me alone," I demanded.

"Okay, I'll do what I can. What is his name again?" He wrote down Joseph's name and occupation and tucked it away in his pocket as I stood there starring out the door. "Well, he must have gone out the kitchen door while you went out the front."

"No," I said as I turned and blankly looked at him, "he's still in the house." I pointed to the latched deadbolt at the top of the back door. "He couldn't have left."

***

Nichols' phone rang as he stumbled out of bed to answer it. "Hello, Nichols here." He listened as Riley told him about Joseph and his late-night call from Jenny. "No man, I don't want to do that. Can't you just leave it alone?" Nichols said with a sigh. "Okay, fine. I'll be there in a few minutes," he said, hanging up.

Nichols sat up on the side of the bed, trying to wake up, as he thought about what had happened the last time he was there. Could he go back? He knew no one was safe there, but how would he tell them without Riley hitting the roof? Would Riley finally have enough of him and tell the sergeant he couldn't handle him anymore? Nichols didn't want to lose Riley as a partner or a friend. He wanted so much to be like Riley, strong and brave.

Nick knew Riley couldn't see the truth around him. Rather, he would find a logical explanation for all the *happenings* at Willow's Dawn and in his quest for answers, something terrible was bound to go wrong.

Nichols chugged a quick cup of instant coffee in hopes of waking up. The under-dissolved grounds felt more like a rock tumbling down into his nervous stomach. He held back the urge to gag and headed out the door.

***

"When Nichols gets here, we'll search the entire house. We'll find him, don't worry," he said, gently placing his hand on my shoulder. "So how long has he been here? Since you called me?" he said, grabbing his notebook and trying to keep all his facts straight.

"No, he showed up while I was waiting for you. When he knocked, I thought it *was* you." By this time, I was so tired and weak from the excitement, I could barely answer his questions. Then, I remembered everything that happened after he left that afternoon. I told him about the cellar deadbolt and then the loud bang and the deadbolt having been unlatched again.

He stood from the table and walked over to the door. "Really? Do you mean this latch? Unlatched? Are you sure it wasn't just your imagination? Or maybe a dream? This latch hasn't opened in years. Look, it's rusted shut," he said, jiggling it back and forth as much as it would go.

"What are you talking about?" I said, evidently mad by this time. I wasn't crazy, and I wasn't making up stories or dreaming. "It's not rusted shut. Try harder," I said, getting up. "Here, let me do it." I grabbed the deadbolt to pull it back, but it wouldn't budge. I tried harder, but it wouldn't come loose. "I don't understand." I looked at Riley with pleading eyes.

"Maybe you should go somewhere for a while. . . a hotel, or something," he stuttered.

"What? Why? No!" I said.

He turned towards the living room and said, "Nichols is here." He walked away and headed for the front door to let his partner in, not even acknowledging my protests.

Nichols nodded to both Riley and I and said, "Well, let's just hurry and get this over with."

***

I sat on the couch while they searched the entire house but came up with nothing. Maybe it was just a dream. I have *had* weird dreams ever since my first night here at Willow's Dawn.

After they finished their search, Nichols sat in a chair directly across from me as Riley sat down next to me on the couch. Nichols rested his head in his hands and then let out a long sigh.

"So, tell me about this man, Joseph. Tell me everything about each time you saw him," Nichols said, sitting back, ready to listen.

I told Nichols and Riley about the day I moved in and then everything that happened tonight. Nichols sighed again. "There hasn't been a groundskeeper here at Willow's Dawn since your grandparent's murder, and the one they had before that was named JD."

"What do you mean murdered? I was told they died a strange death, not murdered. By who? Are they still in jail?"

I couldn't believe what I was hearing, and I slowly started to remember a JD. He was a creepy, tall man with dark, scary eyes. My grandparents loved him. You would have thought he'd hung the moon. He took care of their and Willow's Dawn's every need.

Then, it hit me. "I think I remember him, but vaguely. I do know my grandparents loved him, though. You don't think Joseph is a relative of JD's, do you?"

Nichols looked at Riley and said, "No, I think Joseph is JD."

Riley stood up. "No, now don't do that. That's not possible, and you know it. JD is dead, he hung himself after he killed the Setliff's. JD IS DEAD!" Riley yelled.

"I know he is. I think it's his ghost," Nichols said meekly.

Riley laughed as he said, "You fool, when are you going to stop with all these childhood campfire stories? You're not going to drag Jenny into this. It's ridiculous."

Riley seemed extremely upset, and I didn't understand why since it was just a story. Why was he afraid? Did this have something to do with me? How much did Riley know about my family?

I stood up to defend myself. "What are you talking about?" I yelled. "You tell me my grandparents were murdered, and then you tell me their beloved JD did it. Then, you tell me JD is dead and haunting me?" I sat back down trying not to lose too much control. "You're right, this is ridiculous. There are so many pieces to this puzzle missing. What's going on here? Anyway, Nichols, Joseph is short and scary. JD was tall and scary, and they are about the same age. So, Joseph can't be JD," I said, trying to lay all of the information out in my head.

"How old were you when you visited your grandparents here?" Nichols asked.

"I don't know. Five…six…seven?" I shrugged. "I can't remember much of my time here. It's all kind of blurry."

"So, don't you think it's possible to a young child that a short, old man may appear to be taller than he is? And Riley, haven't you always said that nothing made sense with the murders?"

Nichols' words cut into me, quick and swift. I didn't believe in ghosts, but I also couldn't explain everything that was happening either.

He continued, "What about the cellar latch? Did you know that's where JD hung himself? How do you explain that? Riley?" Nichols shot Riley a look of despair and sighed again. "Okay, earlier this evening after we checked the house, I didn't tell you what happened to me. I was afraid you would report me to headquarters, and they'd commit me or something. But after this, I think you should both know."

He relived the events that took place in the living room and the kitchen and about the cellar door opening. He also mentioned the creepy, male figure staring at him from the attic window. Both Riley and I just sat there, not knowing what to say. At least I knew I wasn't the only one seeing strange things with the cellar door. Not that it was very reassuring.

"Okay, so what do we do? Call a priest?" I said with a chuckle. "I don't believe in ghosts, I don't believe in the devil, and I certainly don't believe in God."

Nichols looked at me with a worried look on his face. "Well, you should, because he's the only one who can help you now."

We sat talking about my family history, and I learned more than I had bargained for. JD wasn't the kind, sweet man my grandparents had said him to be, and in the end, I was right. He was a creepy, old man. My grandparents were secretly plotting to fire him and chase him out of town because of his obsession with Willow's Dawn.

I also found out the real reason she has had so many different owners over the years. They were all chased away, but chased away by what? By the ghost of JD, who introduces himself as Joseph, the groundskeeper? It sounded preposterous.

I didn't know what to believe anymore. Nothing made sense. How could this be happening, as it defied every logical explanation I had found. But as hard as I looked, I couldn't find a way to break Nichols' theory. It may have explained the dreams I have been having and the strange occurrences that kept popping up. All of my troubles could be from hauntings?

As dawn broke and the air turned warmer, I said goodbye to my new confidants and promised I would call at a moment's notice if anything weird happened. They wanted me to go into town and find a hotel room, but this was my house, my grandparent's house. I had to stay and defend it from whatever was happening.

I watched them pull out of the driveway and turned towards the house. *Ghosts?* I thought with a laugh. *He can't be serious*. I couldn't help but glance up towards the attic. Maybe that's what I needed to do. . . take another trip to the attic.

CHAPTER FOUR

Weeks had passed without any signs of strange phenomena. Riley dropped by a few times here and there. It was nice to have someone to talk to along with someone to rely on in case I needed help. I continued to keep busy and search for answers, anything that would explain what was happening. The attic was the most natural place for this to happen.

You could tell that the previous owners had sifted through all of my grandparent's boxes, but everything was still well kept and organized. I had lined up pictures, letters, and bank statements all around me like a massive maze just waiting for the rat to find the cheese. I looked at each pile, not sure where to begin, so I picked up the collection of letters and started my journey into the past.

The letters were beautiful. They were filled with hope and love. The letters were from my grandfather to my grandmother while he was away in the war. They had loved each other very much. If only I could find that kind of bond with someone, but my life was a lost story somewhere in the dark filled with heartache and misery, not hope and love.

Thinking back to when I was five and the brutal car accident that took my parents made a tear well up in my eye. After that, I spent the summers with my loving grandparents here at Willow's Dawn and the rest of the year with my aunt and uncle. Just thinking about that brought back so many unwanted memories. My uncle was an alcoholic and found great pleasure out of punishing me and throwing me against the nearest furniture or walls. My aunt wasn't any better. She knew what he was doing but she was too afraid to do anything about it or possibly even care to do anything about it. Her philosophy was always "better you than me." I wanted to live with my grandparents. I was always so happy when I was here at Willow's Dawn…until…Oh, how I wish I could remember what happened here. Why was I was sent away and never able to return? All I knew was three weeks later, they told me my grandparents had died. Not one person would say to me why or how, but I knew it had something to do with a bad storm down south. I thought it was because I was too young to understand, but as I grew older, still no one would talk about that night or why I was banished.

I set the letters back down and something from the pile of pictures caught my eye. I picked it up, but nothing seemed out of place. It was a picture of Willow's Dawn right after she was finished being built. She had been a wedding gift to my grandparents from my great grandparents. My great grandfather was a very prominent builder in this area, and he got most of his supplies free through friends and other builders.

I was staring at the old black and white picture when the attic window caught my eye, but when I looked closely, there was nothing there. I jumped as I heard the thunder closing in and then someone yelling my name from downstairs. Riley? I smiled as I put the pile of pictures back down and ran down to see who it was.

When I got to the front door, I stopped to check myself in the foyer mirror. *How silly, it's just the detective,* I thought as I checked my hair anyways. When I was finished, I swung open the door.

Riley stood there on the steps in regular clothing. I had never seen him in anything other than his white work shirt and tan slacks. He looked very handsome. From behind his back he pulled out a cheap assortment of wildflowers and what appeared to be—weeds. I smiled.

"Hi, Jenny. I thought I'd drop by to see if everything was still okay and how you were holding up," Riley stuttered. "I thought these would cheer you up." Thrusting the flowers at me as I kindly took them from him.

"Thank you. Things are great, nothing new to report since yesterday." I felt uneasy after saying that. I was actually happy to see him again so soon. "Would you like to come in for coffee or tea? I can tell you about what I've found in the attic."

I moved my body to open the door wider for him to slip through. He followed me to the kitchen where I grabbed a glass of water to use as a vase for my roadside attraction. It was a cute gesture, the same as when a little boy picks flowers from the yard for his mom.

"So, what did you find upstairs?" he asked as he pulled out a chair from the table. "Anything that will help you get to know your family better?"

"Not really," I said, stirring sweetener into our coffees. I had learned from previous visits that the detective had a bit of a sweet tooth. "I did find a lot of letters and pictures from when the house was first being built. Tell me more about what you know and why you are so fascinated by my house." I placed his cup down in front of him and pull out the chair directly across from him. Now it was my turn to interrogate him.

"I personally don't know much about your house. I grew up in the town over. I do remember being in love with it though. There was something magical about Willow's Dawn." His eyes glazed over as he reminisced. He shuffled nervously in his chair and cleared his throat.

"I've only been in the house once. What do you think about the things Nick was saying the other night? About Joseph being JD and your house being haunted?" He looked at me with a stern look on his face while changing the subject. I wasn't sure what I sure say.

"Haunted is such a strong word. Do I feel like I'm being watched? Yes. Do I hear strange noises coming from a completely empty house? Again, yes." I leaned in across the table, as far as I could get to Riley, and whispered, "Sometimes, I think I can hear her breathing."

Riley jerked his body back upright in his chair and composed his thoughts. "When I was young, I had a friend that lived over here. I would come to his house on weekends and we'd hang out. We would stay up late at night and tell ghost stories. His stories always revolved around Willow's Dawn. I know he made them up, but he would scare me, and himself, with the stories."

Now I was enthralled. "What kind of stories? Tell me one."

"Now that's morbid. We're in the house right now and you want me to tell you a ghost story about it?" He placed his hand on his chin and smiled and nodded.

"One of his favorites was the ghosts that walk around the property at night when your grandparents were away. It's like they were guarding it. He said his older brother told him about this time when a bunch of their friends came up one night to look around. As they made their way around the outside of the house, they tried to peer into all the windows to see what they could see. One of his brother's friends came around to the back door," he said motioning to the door behind him, "and he threw a brick through the windowpane, right there on the door. Then, he slipped his hand through to unlock it. Something reached out and touched his hand and whispered, *'Please, come in.'*" Riley smiled as he looked at my wide-eyed stare and continued. "The boys went to the police the next day and the police came out to the house, but the window was fine, no broken glass. The boys said they must have dreamt it because they didn't want to get in trouble for trespassing."

Riley straighten up in his chair and laughed. "Jenny, it's okay. It's only a ghost story. They aren't real. It's just one kid trying to scare another kid."

"How can you be sure it's not true? Something weird has happened almost daily since I moved in. Maybe Nichols and your friend's brother are right. After everything you have heard and seen you aren't the least bit open-minded about something supernatural possibly going on here?"

"I thought you didn't believe in ghosts?"

I let out a long sigh. "I honestly don't know what to believe anymore. But I am open-minded."

Riley thought for a moment. "There is this crazy old lady my old department calls in for weird cases. They call her Madam Zola, one of those physics that help police with missing person's cases. I always thought she was just lucky. Can any of that be real? Can some people see things that others can't? I'm a detective, so I'm skeptical. I can't help it."

I felt defeated. How could I convince him that I wasn't crazy? There was some serious, weird shit going on here. I needed help. "Okay, you win."

"I should probably go. I just wanted to check on you," Riley said standing up and pushing his chair to the table.

I walked him to the door and just stared at him.

"It's going to be okay. We're going to figure everything out." He put his hand to the side of my face and brush a loose strand back.

I put my head down and blushed as he walked to his car and drove away.

I couldn't shake the ghost story Riley had told me. *Just kid's stuff, right?* I thought as I laid down on the couch, turned the TV on, and quickly fell asleep.

CHAPTER FIVE

I awoke to banging on the front door. The TV was off, and the lights were still on. *I must have slept all night,* I thought as I looked at the clock displaying 10 a.m.

Nichols was standing on the porch with the front door propped open when I arrived in the foyer.

"Hello, Jenny. I was hoping you'd be here," he said with a smile. "I just wanted to check on you and make sure everything was still all right. I didn't mean to wake you," he said as I stretched and yawned.

"It's okay, thank you. I really should be up and doing things already. But truly, that was the best sleep I had had in a while."

He nodded and continued, "I know Riley has been by quite a few times to check, but I wanted to come by to say hi, too."

I couldn't hide the fact that Riley's name made me blush, and it was true. I had seen Riley quite often over the past few days, and the thought gave me butterflies like a schoolgirl. "Why thank you, Nichols. Would you like to come in for a cup of coffee?" I asked.

"Oh no, that's fine…I really can't stay, and I don't want to come in." Nichols smiled politely and put his head down in embarrassment. "I just wanted to see if things were okay…" His voice kept trailing off like he forgot what was on his mind.

I walked him down the steps to his car, and he turned to face me. "So…everything is all right, huh?" Nichols stood mesmerized by Willow's Dawn, his face white and his look transparent. "You know when the storm clouds are moving in, that's always when something bad happens."

"Please don't start that again," I begged. "I've been enjoying the past few nights of much-needed rest, and I believe that I have nothing to worry about."

I started wondering if Nichols was even listening to me, as he seemed to be in some sort of a trance just staring up towards the house. I slowly turned my head to follow his gaze to the attic window only in time to see a shadowy figure move away from the window. "Oh God, not again." I felt like I was fighting a battle I'd never win. I was beaten and so tired. I was just up there yesterday, and nothing had been there just me and my mess. My mind started spinning as I realized Nichols was talking to me.

"Yes, I think that's what you should do," he nodded.

"What? Huh?" I came back to reality as I drew my attention off the window.

"A séance. Call someone who can help control this spirit thing you have going on here, or you could just be like all the others and run away."

Nichols knew me well enough by now to know I would never run away. He knew what to say to get me on the edge and ready to fight. "You've got to be kidding me. I would never run away, but a séance? That's nuts. Don't they use those to call upon the dead? I thought you said I had enough dead here already. Why would I want more?" I said with an uneasy laugh.

Nichols laughed at my stupid joke, which only proved just how scared he was also. "Well, not always. Sometimes you can get what they call a medium and what they do is act like a go-between for you and your spirit. You can talk to it and it can talk to you. You can find out what it wants and make it happy, then maybe he will go away for good."

Now it was my turn to laugh. "Isn't that what they call 'making a deal with the devil?' I'm not sure that's such a good idea. It sounds weird and could be a bit dangerous if it is true."

"No, I don't think so. People do it all the time, and what other choice do you have here? And anyway, I thought you didn't believe in the devil," Nichols said, smiling at his new, smart pop shot.

"A week ago, I didn't believe in a lot of things," I frowned. "I don't think Riley will go for this, but I'll ask him about it and see what he says." I pulled out my cell phone and started dialing Riley's number, but before I could finish, Nichols put his hand over my phone.

"No, don't tell Riley. That's not a good idea at all. He thinks he can solve this on his own, and Riley has been fighting this case for nearly twenty years now. He'll never go for it, so please don't call him," Nichols pleaded.

"What do you mean? Fighting this case?" Little things Riley had said to me but never explained started coming back to me. Like why he and Nichols had shown up unannounced the first night and when he had said my house had always been cold. "Did Riley know my grandparents?"

"No, he didn't know them." He was starting to get nervous and uncomfortable with the conversation as he leaned back on the trunk of his car and sighed. "I thought you knew this." Nichols put his hand up over his mouth, looked up, and sighed deeply. "Riley was the lead sheriff for your grandparent's murder case. It was his first big case, but it was never fully solved, and he hasn't been able to let go of it ever since."

"Never solved? But I thought you said JD did it? Now you're saying he didn't do it?" I was getting frustrated with these two. Why wouldn't Riley have told me this? What would be the point of lying and hiding it? I didn't understand.

"No. I mean yes, he did it. Well, I guess he did it. See, that's the problem! Everything is so weird. It just didn't make any sense. He left a note saying he killed the Setliff's, but then wrote on the cellar wall 'Help Me.' It looked like an open-and-shut case but they never really found the murder weapons. They did find what could have been the murder weapons, but they had no blood evidence on them, and that just doesn't happen on a murder/suicide scene," Nichols tried to explain. "Nothing seemed to make sense, but the lead detective said it was open and shut. Now Riley is the lead detective, and he doesn't feel like it's shut."

I sighed loudly. "Well, that's even more reason to tell him. He can be here and maybe he'll learn more about that night or whatever the ghost person tells us. I can't believe I'm agreeing to this," I said, rolling my eyes. "And not to point this out, but I can't even get you inside for a drink. What makes you think you could show up for a séance? Riley needs to be here. If not for himself, then for me."

"You're right. I can't say anything, but you're right." He handed the phone back to me and said, "Call him. Maybe he'll listen to you."

I dialed Riley's number but got no answer and shut the phone. "Okay, now what?" Just as I uttered the words out of my mouth, Riley's car pulled into my driveway. The dark green Mustang pulled to a halt and Riley stepped out of the car. As he waved, he said, "Ah…good you're both here. Jennifer, there's someone I would like you to meet."

Riley went to the passenger side of the car and opened the door. A tall, beautiful, African American woman stepped out of the vehicle. She had deep, brown eyes and wore the most magnificent robe wrapped loosely around her body. Riley smiled as he spoke, "May I introduce Madam Zola? She is the physic medium I told you about. I was hoping she could help us with our problem." The smile on Riley's face made us both burst into laughter. He was finally loosening up.

***

"Hello," she said, smiling warmly at us. "The detective here tells me you have a problem with your house, child?" She took me by the hand and looked into my eyes. "You have had many hardships in your life, a lot of sorrow and sadness. You know many things that could help us help you, but you refused to tell us." She wrinkled her nose. "No, you can't tell us because you don't recall."

I looked at Madam unknowingly, and she turned and walked away towards the house.

As Madam Zola looked at the surroundings, we all watched in amazement. She was eccentric but also had a look of wisdom about her. She played the part well, almost too well, like she was an actress waiting for her next line. I couldn't help but have my reservation towards her, but I trusted Riley immensely. As she walked around the grounds, Riley whispered to us that he had told her nothing about the house or what had happened here twenty years ago and absolutely nothing about what had happened in the last few days.

Riley said he had gone out of town on a case after he left my house yesterday and had mentioned our problem to the detective he was working with. He told Riley that Madam Zola was coming in for a case later that day and suggested he should stay and have a chat with her. Since we were just talking about her, he thought it was a sign and brought her to introduce her to me.

We ran to catch up with her before she disappeared around the back to the gardens.

"The trees here have a lot to tell. They have seen many, many things," she said.

I was taken back by her remark and thought about the day I had moved in. I had that same feeling, but Joseph had stopped me. "Something terrible has happened out here near the veranda, something that changed someone's life." She put her finger into the air, turned towards me, and pointed. "Yours," she said accusingly. They all looked at me, and I just shrugged my shoulders. Nothing I knew of happened that was "terrible." I didn't get any weird feelings out here and all I felt was happiness. Then I remembered, "Well, I was back here the first time I met Joseph."

"Joseph? No, I'm not getting that name. It seems dead to me." She continued looking in circles around the gardens.

"Yes," said Nichols, "that's because it's a dead guy named Joseph."

"No boy, I don't mean that kind of dead. I mean when you say the name, it seems non-existent, not true. You know, dead," she said waving her hand in the air as if dismissing the thought entirely. "There has not been anyone here named Joseph."

The three of us just looked at each other puzzled. Now I thought she was a nut.

"You can think what you want about me, young lady, but I'm telling you, the man you met back here was not named Joseph."

I was shocked. How did Zola know what I was thinking? Maybe giving her a chance was a good idea, as we had nothing better at the moment anyway. We continued holding back behind her so we wouldn't be in the way and so we could talk amongst ourselves.

"Take me to the attic," she demanded as she turned and headed for the kitchen door.

"What was that all about, Jen?" Riley whispered accusingly. "Did you say something to her? Give her some weird sort of body language that only women can see? What?" he said with a laugh.

Madam Zola stopped, turned back towards us, and said, "No, detective. I was just trying to clear up some doubts she has towards me. Now, are you coming, or shall I find it myself?" Madam Zola opened the back door and went inside on her own to start her search. She looked back at us once more as if to say, "I'm waiting," then let the door silently shut behind her. I started my way to the kitchen door and stopped to look back at the boys, waiting for them to catch up.

Riley was just standing there staring at the back door as Nichols and I laughed at the situation. "Well, I guess it would be senseless to hold back anything we're thinking," I said as we followed Madam inside.

The three of us walked into the kitchen giggling like school children but stopped when we saw Madam Zola standing in front of the cellar door. She didn't speak a word as she went to place her hands on the wood. As soon as her fingertips touched it, she drew them back like the door was on fire. We looked at each other too afraid to speak out.

"There's evil down there. Pure evil." She turned away from the door and headed through the living room to the stairwell, trailing her hand along the walls as she went. Nichols cringed as he watched the tips of her fingers and the thought of that night hit him again. When she got to the stairs, she pointed up. We nodded and began to follow her again.

Up in the attic, we noticed that the storm had passed, and the three of us felt a bit of relief and relaxed with our surroundings. We stood there quietly as she made her way around the attic to the window. "There's much sorrow here," she said sadly.

"Sorrow? How can that be? I have seen the shadow of a man, and so has Nichols, on more than one occasion," I protested.

"Yes, it is in every corner up here, unlike the cellar," she started to explain. "You see, it is almost like good versus evil," she said waving her hands all about her. "Heaven and Hell. The ground is the portal to evil, and in most haunted houses, you will find the cellar to be cold, dark and lonely. That is where evil resides. Now, on the other hand, you have the heavens," she said, waving her hand up above her head. "The spirit you have residing in here is not evil, dear child, but good. Although, they are a sorrowful and lonely soul."

Well, that could be true. The only time I had felt fear up here was when the rat tried to kill me. When I thought of that I looked at Riley and said, "Tell that to the rat." He smiled and hugged me close to his side. I was shocked and taken off guard by it, so I pulled away. As I did, he frowned.

"If the spirit here is good, then why is there so much sorrow, and why don't they come and fight the evil for me?" I asked.

"You see, dear child, it's not that easy. Plus, that only happens in the movies," she said with a smile. "The evil is what has caused the sorrow, and this spirit feels weakened by it. The spirit is deeply hurt. I think we should try to contact it and find out what happened. It may help us find out more about the evil," Madam explained. "I'll be back. I brought something that may help us with the situation." With that, she was down the stairs and out the front door.

We all looked at each other, waiting for the other ones to say something first, but no one wanted to take the step. I looked out the window and saw Madam at Riley's car. She opened the door, took out a rectangular object, and headed back towards the house, never once looking at the attic window. She stopped and waved at me anyway.

"How does she do that?" I said in amazement, and the guys just laughed.

Madam walked back up the attic stairs and sat down on the floor. "Okay, I need everyone to form a circle," she said as she placed the Ouija board in front of her. "Gather around the board, knees touching please."

The three of us sat down where she told us to and silently looked at each other unknowingly, waiting for her next command.

"Don't be afraid and don't doubt. There is no room for doubt. Do not consider this a séance. It's just a simple question and answer session if you will," she said with a smile.

She straightened her back and sat as tall as possible as she continued, "Now everyone relax. You will not have to do anything, but if you have a specific question, you can tell me…or think it," she said with a wink and a coy smile on her face, "and I will ask for the answer."

She then pulled out a triangular piece of wood and placed it in the middle of the board. "Everyone, place your two index fingers loosely on the planchette and concentrate." She waited for everyone to follow her directions before she continued. "I said concentrate," she said, looking at Riley. Nichols snickered at Riley and Madam turned and frowned at him, too. "Now, I am going to ask a few questions, and hopefully, the spirit will use the board to answer us." She looked around at everyone until she was satisfied and then closed her eyes. "Oh, spirit of sorrow, answer us please. We come to you in search of answers for this poor, dear child. Are you here with us?" We all sat quietly and watched the triangular pointer. Slowly, I started to feel it move under my fingers as it made its way slowly over to the 'yes' on the board. Madam continued, "Good, thank you for speaking with us. What is your name? Who are you?" The pointer started to shake but not move. "Please, we are only here to help. Who are you?" The arrow started its way across the board.

e -l -o -u -i -s -e

"Elouise? Is this Elouise?" Madam asked.

"Elouise was my grandmother! Grandma, is that you?" I yelled.

"Quiet, I will ask the questions! Is this Elouise, Jennifer's grandmother?" The pointer started moving again, this time a little faster. e-l-o -u-i-s-e. "Is this Elouise?" she asked again, and the arrow went back. e-l-o-u-i-s-e. "Who is this? Is this Elouise?" The pointer darter across the board to the word 'No,' then kept circling the board, going faster and faster until our fingers flew off of the planchette, spelling out Elouise over and over again. "Elouise, Elouise, Elouise, Elouise, Elouise, Elouise, Elouise, Elouise." The pointer was going so fast we couldn't even see the letters it was forming. The temperature dropped hard and fast, and the wind ripped through the attic from somewhere around us. Madam quickly broke the circle and stood up, yelling, "Enough!"

The pointer stopped, and all went quiet.

"What the hell was that?" Riley yelled. All I could do was sob. What was happening? If that wasn't my grandmother, then who was it? This time I welcomed Riley's arms around me as they let me lay there and cry for a moment before Madam continued.

"Well, whoever that was seemed concerned about your late grandmother. There is nothing more we can do today. I'll be back on the weekend for a proper examination." She turned to Nichols and said, "Will you take me home? I don't think he needs to be leaving her alone just yet." She turned to Riley and said, "Stay with her and don't let her out of your sight. I have a bad feeling that this evil spirit wants her for something."

Riley and I walked Nichols and Madam out to the car. I hugged her and thanked her for all she had done tonight and promised not to doubt her again. She smiled and just waved her hand, totally dismissing the thought as we watched them drive away.

CHAPTER SIX

The two of us headed back into the house and Riley shut the door behind us. I sat down on the couch and let out a long sigh, then slowly kicked my shoes off so I could curl my feet up under me. I was exhausted. Riley sat at the opposite end of the couch with his head propped in his hand.

"What's wrong?" he asked. "Tired?"

"Yes. Tired, worn out, sad, mentally and physically exhausted. You name it, I'm it. Plus, my feet hurt," I said with a whine.

Riley looked at me and smiled. "Here, give me your feet," he said, patting his lap.

I laughed nervously and extended my feet. "You're not going to touch those smelly things, are you?"

"Yes. Yes, I am," he said with a big smile and a nod. "And you're going to lay here and enjoy it."

He began to rub my feet and I relaxed a bit. I drifted off in my thoughts and realized this whole situation was getting worse. Madam said the presence in the basement was evil. What would happen if it comes out of the cellar? So far it has only teased and tortured, how would it go now? I was still perplexed about who Joseph was. Was he good or evil? Something was strange about the way he acted and his whole story was odd. My grandparents wanted to get rid of him because he was obsessed with this house. But loving a home, is that such a bad thing? Maybe Joseph is the troubled spirit in the attic, or perhaps he was the evil spirit in the cellar. I sighed loudly out of frustration again.

Riley could see that I was beginning to tense up again, so he leaned his head in a little farther towards my feet and said, "Wow, they do stink." He wrinkled up his nose and turned to smile at me.

I picked up one of the couch pillows, threw it at him, and he yelled, "Hey, watch it. You'll mess up my hair," as he patted down what little hair he had on top of his head. We both laughed at his remark and relaxed a little more. "So," he started, "are you going to be able to go upstairs and pack by yourself?"

I looked at him, not knowing how to answer his question. "What do you mean?" I knew what he meant, but I didn't feel like starting another *time-to-go-to-a-hotel* fight.

Riley was afraid of where this was going to go. "Well, I thought you could come stay with me until the weekend. I have a guest room. Madam Zola told me not to let you out of my sight, right? Anyway, there's someone whom I would like you to meet back home. I think she'd like you. You're both feisty, little blondes."

I just stared at him in shock. I couldn't believe it. Married? But I thought, how could he? "No thank you," I said, trying to be polite as I lifted my feet from his lap. "I'm not leaving my house. We've been through this before."

Riley looked a little hurt by the removal of my feet and said, "I don't believe I have ever met anyone as stubborn as you are. You heard what she said. You've got at least two spirits in this house, and one of them just may try to hurt you. Why in the world would you want to stay here?"

I looked at him as my mind raced. I didn't understand. Was it just the cop in him wanting to protect me? Was I getting the wrong signals from him? What about the flowers and the way he looked at me?

"Okay, I have a better idea. Why don't you go pick her up and bring her here? You can stay in one of my guest rooms or are you too afraid to stay here at night?"

I didn't want to meet her, but what else were my choices? I didn't want to stay alone, and I didn't want to leave. I would just have to be polite and pretend whatever I was feeling for Riley was friendship and admiration, nothing more.

"I guess that would work. Okay, we'll go get her and stay here. It can be like a sleepover. Hey, we could watch old movies all night. She loves old cop movies. I'll make popcorn" Riley said.

His words started to fade out of my ears. Oh joy, I thought as I smiled.

He continued, "And we could tell ghost stories." He laughed hysterically over that one even though it was only moderately funny. "Jenny? You're not smiling. Are you ok? You don't mind the extra company, do you?"

I tuned back into his sleepover plans, "No, it's fine. Really, the more, the merrier," I lied.

"Well, put your shoes on and let's go. I want to get back here before dark," he said, standing up and grabbing his coat.

I slowly slipped my shoes back on with about as much enthusiasm as a sloth eating his food and smiled at him, "Ok, I'm ready. Let's go."

***

We pulled up in front of Riley's house and he turned off the ignition. "You wait here. It will only take a moment," he said, getting out of the car.

"Should I get in the back?" I yelled. Not wanting to cause problems between them, I opened the door to get out, but he stopped me.

"Oh no, don't worry about it. I don't let her sit up front. She always tries to climb in my lap, and I can't drive straight." Riley laughed as he disappeared inside his house.

I just sat there, not knowing what to do. *Surely, he was joking*, I thought. As I sat there trying to figure out what my first words to this mystery woman would be, I decided that this was a bad idea. With how awkward this was, I should have never agreed to it.

Just then, the back door of the police cruiser opened. I never saw them come out of the house. I turned in my seat, smiled, and then broke into laughter as I faced the most beautiful golden dog I had ever seen. She leaned up and licked me in my face as Riley got in. "Good, she likes you. I knew she would," he said with a proud smile on his face. "Jenny, this is Baby. Baby, this is Jenny," he said, introducing us like two humans. I stared at Baby and just laughed, hard and uncontrollably, I couldn't stop.

"I thought, oh my," I gagged for air, "but you said, and then I thought." I couldn't stop laughing long enough to form a complete sentence.

A look of surprised understanding washed over Riley's face as he blushed and began laughing, too. "You thought Baby was a person?"

I still couldn't stop laughing, so I nodded my head instead and reached out to stroke poor Baby's fur. She was stunning. I couldn't have been happier to meet her. "Sorry, I'm not that kind of guy. I can't have feelings for two women," he said, reaching out and touching my cheek as he leaned in closer to try to kiss me, but I shyly lowered my face away from him.

I stopped laughing and straightened up in the seat. "We should be heading back. It's getting dark." I smiled at Riley as the butterflies swarmed in my stomach. Right now, nothing could destroy what I was feeling, not even Joseph.

He smiled warmly and nodded.

***

When we returned to Willow's Dawn, we set up a cozy bed for Baby in front of the fireplace and we sat on the couch and watched her cuddled up in it. Somehow, I felt more secure with her there between me and the kitchen entryway. She seemed pretty at ease herself as we both started to drift off to sleep.

When I woke, the TV was still on and Riley was asleep on the other end of the couch, so I quietly got up as not to wake him and made my way into the kitchen to make a cup of coffee. Everything seemed fine. I checked the kitchen and cellar doors and they were both still dead-bolted. I smiled to myself as I thought of how nice it would be to lay and relax in a nice, hot bath of bubbles.

I grabbed my coffee and quietly headed towards the stairs. When I entered the living room, Baby raised her head and cocked it to look at me, so I patted my hand to my hip and motioned for her to follow me. You could hear the quiet thumping of her tail against the floor as she laid there and thought about getting up. Her old bones finally got the strength to do so and we proceeded up the stairs. You could tell how old she was by her limped climb up the stairs. Poor old girl. I had to wonder if I was taking too much advantage of her kindness. She noticed me watching her, and she wagged her tail and nudged me in the back of the leg as if she was trying to get me to move along. I laughed and finished the hike.

I found my candles and lit them in a circle around my bath. I slowly seeped into the hot, soapy water as Baby curled up by the door.

There I was, standing at the edge of the cliff again, the fresh, autumn air flowing through my hair as I looked out towards the ocean. The wind whipped through my dress as a sense of peace washed over me. I heard from a distance someone call my name. I turned around and saw it was Riley smiling and waving to me from the veranda. I waved back as he started walking towards me. I could see the wind blow through his white work shirt. I closed my eyes and thanked God for all the happiness that was in my life.

As Riley approached me, I felt his arms encircle me like a perfect vine to its rose. I could feel his breath on my neck and in my ear, but something felt strange. An overwhelming fear came over me as I broke free from his grip. His face had changed into Joseph, now standing before me. The thunder roared and I could feel the sting of the lighting as it hit a tree in the not-too-far distance. I stared into the face of this mad man as he said, "Now, you die too." He pushed me over the side of the cliff, and I fell and fell.

I woke up with a sudden jerk and noticed my bath water was cold. *I wonder how long I've been in here,* I thought. I suppose long enough for Baby to give up on me, as she was no longer asleep by the bathroom door.

I sat on the edge of the tub trying to recover from my latest dream. This one was different though because I didn't wake up with the impending feeling of doom as I usually would. I shook it off and grabbed my robe.

As I headed down the stairs, everything was quiet. I knew when I went up, I had left the TV on, but now I couldn't even hear that.

I walked into the living room, and noticed Riley or Baby weren't there. I wonder where those two went? I looked out the front window, and his Mustang was still sitting in the drive. A rush of relief passed over me, and I smiled.

I could smell the freshly brewed coffee coming from the kitchen. *Wow, he is a good man*, I thought as I walked towards the smell of my lifeline.

When I rounded the corner to the kitchen, my heart stopped.

The cellar door was open.

I called out for Riley but didn't get an answer. I walked closer to the door and called out again, and this time I heard a small, faint whimper. Baby! Somehow, she must have gotten down there. Maybe Riley was down there hurt, and she followed him. I had many thoughts racing through my mind. All I wanted to do was get to them. I grabbed the flashlight and headed down the stairs.

Halfway down the steps, I found the string for the light and pulled it. The bulb flickered and shot out a bright light, then blew with a loud POP. Thank goodness I still had my flashlight in my pocket, so I continued my way down to the cold, dark cellar.

I called out for Riley but still no answer. Only Baby's whimpering reached my ears. At the bottom of the steps, I shined the light through the entire dwelling but saw nothing. I called for Baby and then followed the sound of her pain. I ended up on the far end of the cellar far away from the steps. I was terrified. There was nothing here: no Baby nor Riley. I heard a noise at the other end of the cellar and quickly turned to shine my light. I then heard louder whimpering and scratching behind me. I turned back around and saw the faint outline of a door. Baby must be in there, but how?

"Riley?" I screamed, grabbed the door handle to swing it open, and saw Joseph standing there with an ax and a blood-covered Baby lying at his feet. I screamed and cried and tried to run away, but Joseph's grimy, bloody hands grab me by the shoulders. I couldn't get away. I screamed for Riley over and over again and eventually heard Riley yell my name from upstairs. Joseph looked towards the stairwell and said, "I'm not through with you yet." Then, he disappeared.

I woke up to Riley and Baby standing over me on the couch. Riley was shaking me, and Baby was whimpering.

"There you are. It's okay, you're safe. It's just me. You fell asleep a little while ago, and I didn't want to wake you and move you, so I let you just sleep here," he said wiping the sweat from my brow with his handkerchief, "That must have been some dream. We couldn't wake you, and you just kept screaming for us. Do you want to talk about it?"

I just stared at Riley. How could I tell him about my dream, knowing it would break his heart? I pulled myself into a ball and sat at the far end of the couch, holding my knees tight and rocking back and forth as the world faded out from around me.

CHAPTER SEVEN

I sat on the veranda watching Riley and Baby play. The night passed without any significant problems as I slept curled up in Riley's arms on the couch while Baby laid on her mat by the fireplace. It was the best sleep I'd had in weeks.

Tomorrow Madam was returning for the séance, and I could hardly wait for this ordeal to end. I couldn't shake the dream I had the day before. It was so real, almost like an omen. Was Joseph connecting with me? Was Madam right? Should I fear for my life? What of Riley's life, was he safe?

As Riley continued throwing the ball around, I saw Baby getting closer and closer to the edge of the cliff. I yelled out for Riley to watch her and keep her closer to the veranda and he rolled his eyes at me and called back, "Yes mommy," and stuck out his tongue.

"Just be careful," I said, just like my grandparents used to do with me.

Riley laughed. "She's a dog, don't worry. They have a knack of knowing when they are in danger, so she'll be fine."

Those words only made me think of the cellar. I hoped he was right for the sake of us all. I sat out in the open air and I could almost smell the putrid rot that was protruding from the cellar. I couldn't help but wonder what was down there.

Riley noticed the disheartened look on my face and came to sit with me.

"What happened in your dream? You need to tell me. You haven't been the same person all day and I would like the opportunity to help you through it. Don't you trust me?" he pleaded with his eyes. "Something tells me that I have the right to know." He sat there looking at me, waiting for my response. He knew he had won. How could I not tell him now?

I just looked away as the tears filled my eyes because he was right. It concerned him and he needed to know. I cleared my throat and began to recall my dream, starting with my trip into the kitchen and then taking Baby with me for my bath. "Oh, thanks. And you just left me down there all alone?" he said, smiling. I tried to smile but couldn't and just continued with my story. By the time I got to the part of the dream with him, I felt it would be better to skip it. I wasn't sure how he would react or what he would think of me after, so I just said I fell asleep and woke up to no Baby. He could tell I was leaving stuff out but was gracious enough to let it slide.

I told him of the trip down to the cellar and what was behind the door. I could see the pain in his eyes as he assured me that nothing like that would ever happen. "I'll tell you of a dream I had last night if you think it will make you feel better." he said, happily as he pulled me closer. I smiled back and nodded.

He slid his arms around me as he began telling of his dream, and I grinned at the dreamy look in his eye. He looked like a little boy getting his favorite toy at Christmas. "Now remember, you have no control over what you dream about, okay? Hm… On second thought, maybe I shouldn't tell you. You might run me off," he said, leaning back and peering out at me.

That only made me want to hear it more. I knew he must have dreamt about me, and I couldn't wait to seep into his fantasy right along with him.

"Tell me, please," I said, smiling sweetly back at him. "Don't make me beg."

He smirked as he continued, "Well, I was on my way home from work. I was so tired, but I remember feeling happy and excited." He started to blush. "I realized I was heading here to Willow's Dawn instead of my place. I was coming home." He smiled, and I could feel his arms tighten around me as he was swept away back into his dream. "When I pulled into the driveway, I got out, came around back, and saw you. You looked so beautiful that I was speechless. You were standing at the edge of the cliff, and the cool, autumn wind was blowing through your hair." He stopped for a moment to catch his breath, but I couldn't find mine. I was terrified, and I didn't want him to go on. It was just like my dream. . . how could it be? "But then while I was holding you, you just vanished."

I jumped up and backed away from him shaking my head. I didn't know what I should say. Yes, it was a beautiful dream and I had felt it too, but then, I started crying. He ran for me and I just let out a scream as I turned towards the house. "Leave me alone!" I demanded. "What do you want from me?" I yelled and fell to the ground. Riley dropped to his knees beside me and tried to cradle me, but I fought him off. I couldn't let him get any closer to me. I couldn't put him in danger, too.

I told Riley the parts of my dream that I had left out, and he just stared at me in disbelief.

"I know what we have to do. We have to go down there," he said shakily.

I nodded and rose from the ground. He was right. We had to fight, and we couldn't waste another day waiting for Madam Zola. We had to go now, as our sanity depended on it. I grabbed Baby by the collar, and we headed into the house.

***

We stood in the kitchen looking at the cellar door for what felt like an eternity. After what had happened in our dreams, we decided to lock Baby in the upstairs bathroom. She didn't need to follow us down there. She was heartbroken and scratched and howled at the door, but we wanted to keep her safe.

Riley brought the crowbar for the rusted deadbolt, but when he tried to pry it open, the lock slipped right out of place. We looked at each other in disbelief and then he took my hand and asked if I was ready. When I nodded yes, he slowly turned the handle and opened the cellar door.

The smell is what hit us first. It was like rotting roadkill left out in the hot, Georgia midday sun. I turned my head and gagged. "Are you okay?" he asked. "Yes," I lied.

We walked hand in hand down the cellar stairs.

"Riley?" I whispered.

"Yeah, babe?" he responded.

"Don't let go."

He held my hand tighter as if to reassure me. I knew going down here was a bad idea. Still, it was something that we had to, since it wasn't just me anymore. Now he wanted Riley and his dog, too. Maybe it was because he was the lead sheriff so many years ago, or perhaps because whoever this was didn't want me to ever to find happiness.

"Now remember," he stated, "most of what you see down here isn't real. It can't be. It's just a spirit."

"But what about what Madam Zola said?" I protested.

"She can't be right. This can't be real," he said.

I didn't know if he was trying to convince himself or me what he said was true, but I wasn't so sure I bought it, and I don't think he did either.

When we got to the middle of the stairwell, he fumbled for the string. This time, the cellar walkway lit up as the light swayed back and forth, lighting up each part of the cellar systematically. Everything was so quiet down here. Your imagination could have a field day if you stopped long enough to think about it.

With every step we took, the stairs cried out in anguish, almost as if pleading for us not to go any further. Riley turned to me and gave me a reassuring smile as we approached that final step.

***

The cellar was the only place in the house that wasn't finished when building. I didn't know why, but I remembered my grandma always getting onto my granddad about it. He would always respond with, "If you want it to be safe, it will take time." I never knew what he was working on down here because I was not allowed to go any farther than the kitchen door to talk to him. JD was always down there with him while he worked, but he was such a klutz my grandfather would constantly send him upstairs and out of his way. It hurt JD when he would do that to him. Sometimes my grandfather would scream bad names at him, and JD would go out behind the barn and cry. I silently wondered if this was part of the reason why he killed them.

At the end of the steps, there were two vertical support beams on each side. They felt damp as I lightly ran my fingertips across one of them. The cellar itself was huge. It seemed to span the entire length of the house. We first walked over to where the door was in my dream, but it wasn't there. Riley said since I had never been down here, I wouldn't know what the cellar looked like properly. What I had seen was all just a dream. But so far, everything else was the same. I shrugged it off to him being right again.

The walls that surrounded the cellar were made of cold cement blocks, which brought in the cold from outside. Maybe this was why the kitchen was always so cold. There were spots on the floor that were not cemented in, almost like an underground tunnel that gave the whole cellar a dungeon-type feel. On the far wall, there were rows of shovels and rakes for gardening along with a relatively new looking ax. I pointed it out to Riley, and he let go of my hand to pick it up to have a closer look. The original price tag was still on it to expose the price from twenty-some-odd years ago.

"Well, that's a good sign," he said, laughing. "It looks brand new."

I felt a lot better with knowing this because it looked just like the ax from my dream, only a lot cleaner. I was starting to feel more at ease and not as fearful until I noticed a baby doll over in a far corner. I let out a gasp and ran over to her. "My baby doll!" I exclaimed. Riley looked over at me and smiled. She was all worn and dirty and her once beautiful porcelain face was cracked and broken. *How sad*, I thought as I stroked her tiny face.

"Did you leave her down here when you were playing?" he asked.

"No, I was never allowed down here. I lost her one summer and never found her. I wonder how she got down here?"

I was starting to get that same strange feeling I had in my dream. "Riley, I think we should go back upstairs." I turned around. "Riley?" I looked all around me and couldn't see him. "Riley?" Nothing. "RILEY!" I screamed.

Oh no, where did he go? I ran under the stairs to the other side of the cellar, but he wasn't there either. I ran back to the cellar steps and called for him again. "RILEY!"

Still no answer.

He wouldn't have gone upstairs without me. He wouldn't leave me. I didn't know what to do. I ran up the cellar steps and into the kitchen and again screamed, "RILEY!" The cellar door slammed shut, and the deadbolt locked into place. I banged on the door as hard as I could, screaming Riley's name. The deadbolt wouldn't budge. I couldn't get back in. I fell to the floor, crying Riley's name. How was I going to save him now?

I picked up the phone and called Nichols.

CHAPTER EIGHT

I stood in front of the cellar door wishing for it to open. I had to get back down there to Riley. I tried the deadbolt again, but it seemed to be welded shut. I felt the tremble of the windows and realized another storm had moved in, bringing along the cold. It was so cold again, I shivered as I grabbed my sweater off the back of the kitchen chair, and I turned back to bang on the cellar door again feverishly.

"Let me in!" I cried.

I was somewhat surprised how fast Nichols showed up at my house. I could only imagine that he was sworn to protect his partner and wasn't about to lose him to these now real-life childhood campfire stories. I never heard his car pull up in the storm before he banged on the kitchen door. I ran to let him in.

"I'm so happy to see you. I almost didn't think you would come," I said in a shaky voice. "I thought you would bring Madam Zola with you. Where is she?" I asked.

"I didn't call, I just came over as quick as I could. We have to save Riley before he's gone for good," he said wearily.

"I'm hoping that we're not already too late for that. There was nothing down there, and I didn't even hear a sound before he was gone. It's almost as if he just vanished into thin air."

I told Nichols everything he had missed: the dreams we both had, our trip to the cellar, and my missing doll. I tried not to leave anything out.

"I know Riley wants to solve this and get it behind him, but what you two did was completely stupid. What were you thinking going off by yourselves down there?" He was starting to sound more like a father than the scared, little rookie cop we all knew and loved. "The house only wants you, and now you went and dragged your little boyfriend into it all and messed it all up! All our work ruined. Years of studying this house, years of watching him run around in circles, years of torment all for what? For some pretty little floozy to come in here and bring the whole house down."

I was confused. What was he saying? I had never heard him talk this way. He looked up to Riley and valued his every thought. Now, he was demoted to my little boyfriend?

"Nick, I don't understand. What are you talking about?" My eyes filled with tears as I pleaded with him. "Why are you acting this way?"

Nichols had a glazed look over his eyes as he looked at the cellar door. "Nichols?" I questioned. He turned towards me and smiled.

"I'm sorry, I didn't mean for this to come out that way. I hope you can understand the amount of stress this can put one under. My partner, my friend, has been taken by a house." He stared at me, waiting for my approval. "You must understand, right?"

I did understand. I understood that he would be stressed, but I didn't know how he could change character like this. How could he go from not wanting to get anywhere near the house to *this*? It was like having a conversation with two different people. Something wasn't right about Nichols, and I didn't want to trust him. I nodded silently to him, not knowing what to say.

"Well, this is strange. I've been here for more than five minutes, and you haven't offered me a cup of coffee," he said with a smile.

Coffee? How was I supposed to think of coffee right now? I wanted back in the cellar, I wanted Riley. "I'll make a pot." I turned only slightly away from him, as I was too afraid to turn my back completely.

I sat and watched Nichols drink his coffee, but the aroma was starting to make me sick, so I excused myself and went upstairs to the bathroom where Baby was. I felt a little bit better for her because she had finally stopped crying and scratching to get out. I thought about not disturbing her for fear that it would wind her up again, but I was so nauseous I had no choice.

I slowly opened the door, so I wouldn't hit her, and checked around the door frame. She wasn't in front of the door, so I slowly walked in. Where was she? The bathroom wasn't that big, but the toilet and shower area were separated by a divider, so I walked in and peered behind the wall. My heart dropped.

"Where is she?" I said out loud.

I quietly pulled back the shower curtain and began to cry. First Riley and now Baby. How can they just vanish like this? Maybe somehow, she got out of the bathroom and was asleep in my room. I cautiously went back to the bathroom door, peered around the corner, and quietly called her name so Nichols wouldn't hear. She didn't come. I raced into my room and looked on the bed, under the bed, anywhere I felt a dog would go.

"Baby? Where are you, girl? Come on, come to me," I quietly called.

My closet door sat slightly opened, and I saw a shadow slightly move. I smiled as a sigh of relief washed over me.

"Baby!" I said as I ran over and flung it open.

Nichols was standing there with a cold smile on his face, "Nope, sorry. Try again."

His eyes were as black as night, and his whole facial features seemed to have changed. His clothes were all tattered and torn, and he reeked of alcohol. His voice broke as he spoke to me.

"Lose something, Miss? Maybe you should have a nice lie-down, wouldn't that be something nice?" He said as he swung the ax into his other hand with a laugh and lunged towards me.

I let out a scream and ran towards the doorway in a full sprint, barely missing his grasp. I ran down the long hallway that seemed to go on forever. The faster I ran, the longer it got, as if the house was conforming with my every move.

I turned and raced down the stairs but tripped and fell end over end until I stopped and slid to the bottom. I stood up to run, but my foot caved under me. It must have broken in the fall. I looked back up the stairs and didn't see Nichols, so I quietly pulled myself to the closet to hide. I was getting light-headed and the pain that was shooting through my leg wasn't nearly as bad as the pain in my head. I slowly drifted off into the darkness.

***

The rain was pounding hard on the windows when I awoke from my catatonic slumber. Where am I? As my eyes started to focus on the darkness, I could see that I wasn't in my bedroom anymore. I sat up with a jerk, feeling a searing pain in my leg as I slowly remembered what was happening. There was a man in my house, and he was trying to kill me. Riley. I had to get to Riley, but I was too afraid to move. I didn't know how long I was hiding or where Nichols was now, but then, I heard him.

"Where are you, you stupid bitch? I'm going to find you, and when I do, I'm going to rip your damned head off," Nichols yelled. "Come out, now, or I'll kill Riley and his stupid dog."

I was frantic. What did he mean? Were they still alive, or was it just a trick to get me to disclose my hiding place?

I could tell he wasn't too far off from where I was hiding. I needed to get to the attic, but I couldn't say precisely where his voice was coming from. I heard his footsteps pound pass the doorway and on to the kitchen.

"Oh, so now you think you're smart. I know you're down there," I heard him yell down the cellar stairs.

The deadbolt was unlocked. I thought about running to the kitchen and shutting Nick in, but I knew Riley was still down there, and if he were still alive, I would never be able to save him. I quietly opened my refuge door so that I could peek out. When I didn't see him, I carefully slid out of the closet and pulled myself up the long stairwell. I could still hear Nichols down in the cellar throwing things and searching for me, so I knew I still had a little time.

When I finally reached the hallway, I looked up at the attic door. I was so close. I tried to stand so I could grab the stairs and pull them down, but my leg wouldn't hold my weight. I threw my hands over my face and cried, but then I heard the creak of the attic door. I looked up and saw the attic stairs quietly descending towards me. I grabbed hold of the bottom stair and started pulling my way up to safety.

I pulled the attic stairs up behind me and shut the door, then looked around the room and smiled. I said thank you to whoever it was that had decided to help me.

"Who are you?" I asked but got no reply.

I wondered if they knew if Riley and Baby were all right. I turned my head towards a sliding whoosh sound I heard and saw Madam's Ouija board still on the floor. I thought back and remembered her picking it up and taking it with her, so how could it even be here?

I pulled my way over to it and saw the planchette sitting on the word yes.

"Yes. Yes, what?" I asked the air.

I tried to wrack my brain of anything I might have said since I was up here, then I let out a small cry as a single tear rolled down my cheek. I moved the planchette back to the middle of the board and asked again.

"Are Riley and Baby okay?" I observed the board, and nothing seemed to happen. My heart sank as I placed my fingertips onto the corners of the planchette and asked again, "Are Riley and Baby okay?" I felt a trembling in my fingers as I watched it slide towards the yes. "Thank you, thank you," was all I could say.

***

I wasn't sure how much time had passed while I was up in the attic. The storm had disappeared, and the sun was shining through the attic window. I must have fallen asleep again. I sighed, pulled myself over to the window, and looked down on Nichols's car. Was it daytime, almost nighttime? I was so confused. Everything seemed to be running together.

I heard the creak of the attic stairs lowering. I panicked and dragged myself behind a piece of furniture covered by a sheet so I could hide my body the best that I could. He found me, I cried silently. Nowhere to run, nowhere to hide. I tried not to whimper as I heard Nichols call up the steps.

"Jennifer? Are you up there?" he called.

I heard the faint voice of someone else but couldn't make it out. I heard Nichols talking to them. "I don't know where she is. I told her I'd be right over, but then everything went wrong from there. Jenny!" he called again.

"Here, let me try. I know she's up there," I heard Madam Zola say. "Jenny, what's wrong? Come out and talk to us. Why did you call Nichols, and what happened to Riley?" she said in a caring, motherly voice.

I carefully eased my head out from under the sheet. "Madam? Is that you?" I said in a whisper.

I heard feet bounding up the attic stairs and then saw Nichols and began screaming. Nichols stopped and stared at me while Madam made her way over and grabbed me by the shoulders. I continued staring and screaming at Nichols as she shook me back and forth.

"Jenny? Jenny? What is it? It's us, calm down," she said in an even, friendly tone. She tried to block my way from looking at Nichols, but I kept my eye on him as she sat before me stroking my hair and trying to calm me down. "It's ok dear child, just relax. Nothing's going to hurt you now. There's no one here, just us."

I stopped screaming and Nichols started walking towards me again. I grabbed a lampstand and pushed Madam away, then stood up on my hurt leg and cried towards Nichols.

"Leave me alone! You come any closer and I'll kill you," I said shaking the lamp at him.

Nichols put up his hands. "Whoa now, what's wrong, Jenny? It's just me. Please put that lamp down. I'm not here to hurt you."

I lunged towards Nichols with the lamp, and Madam grabbed hold of me while he grabbed the light. I started screaming again and kicked out at Nichols like a wild animal.

"My God Jenny, what's gotten into you?" he screamed back at me.

"You, you took Riley and Baby! You tried to kill me!" I looked at Madam Zola and cried, "Please don't believe him. He was here, he was different. Nick was acting like Joseph, and he smelled like the horrid cellar."

Madam Zola looked at me, nodded her head, and said, "It's this house, Jenny. Stop and listen to me. Please trust me."

I finally stopped struggling and fell from my hurt leg. I pushed myself into the corner where I held on to the lamp. "I'm listening," I said, never taking my eyes off of the man standing before me.

"He called me right after he got off the phone with you, and I told him to come out there and get me, not to go to the house alone. It is a good hour's drive from here, and he made it in record time. So, I know he has not been here until now. On our way here, the tire blew out and it took a little while to get it changed. I felt a presence trying to keep us away. I knew something terrible was happening here, but I promise you, whatever you saw, whoever it was, it was not Nichols."

She just stared at me waiting for me to answer. I was so scared. If this house could do that, then how would we ever know who to believe and who not to? I sat in the corner and cried, then said, "He has Riley. I want that bastard gone!"

Madam nodded her head and said, "Let's get started."

CHAPTER NINE

I felt a little safer after talking with Nichols for a while. It was just the house playing tricks on me. Madam Zola said the evil was not quite strong enough to manifest and cause me any harm. Its only defense right now was to scare me and hope I would leave or even take my own life. It was gaining strength the longer we waited, but for now, Riley was safe somewhere. We just had to find the spirit's most energetic spot, and we would find them both.

In the past two days, Madam Zola had done some investigation work of her own. When she left here that night in the attic, she had taken a picture of Willow's Dawn and a few other personal items she had seen. I was so upset that night, I never even noticed.

She called upon the spirit of my grandmother, who was at rest peacefully, which made me smile. Joseph was not the evil man they had thought he was in the end. The house was evil. It overtook him and made him do everything. All Joseph had wanted to do was take care of me and my grandparents, but he failed. Madam Zola couldn't tell me anything about my grandfather. It was all very shady. When she tried to contact him, something was blocking the way. She didn't understand why. All Madam knew was there was something out of the ordinary when she tried to talk to my grandmother about it and her spirit vanished.

Willow's Dawn was built on "unholy" ground and was taken over by evil before they had even finished building her. No one knew why or what had been here before Willow's Dawn. No grave markers, no cemetery, no records had ever been found.

Madam didn't know for sure, but she suspected the sorrowful spirit in the attic was Joseph, and as long as there was a pain in this house, he would not be at peace. The only way he would be at peace was to find the evil and terminate it. Then, Joseph could move on and Riley and Baby would come back.

Nichols and I just stared at Madam. That sounded easier said than done.

***

Madam placed the candles in the shape of a pentagram around the kitchen table. She said the spirit would have to leave the cellar, as it had already done before, and enter the pentagram. Once inside, she could get it into the board and then we would chop it up, burn it and bury it. That was the only way to be rid of the spirit.

She then lowered her head and spoke quietly, "I am afraid, dear child, that you are the center of this problem. The house wants you. When we first met, I told you something life-changing happened to you out by the veranda. Do you remember that?" I nodded as she continued. "Before this can work, we need to find out what that change was." I looked at her, puzzled.

"I told you, I don't remember. All I have are good memories of my summers here, so I don't know how I can help you. I just don't remember," I promised.

"I know you don't know, child. That is why I have brought this," she said, pulling from her pocket a large ruby stone dangling from a chain. It was beautiful, and mesmerizing. She continued, "I'm going to put you under, and I'm going to take you back to that last summer. The last summer you were here at Willow's Dawn."

I shifted uneasily in my chair. "That doesn't sound like a good idea to me."

Madam and Nichols looked at each other as Nichols grabbed my hand and gave it a quick squeeze with a wink. "It will be okay," Madam said in a matter-of-fact tone. "We are here to make sure nothing happens. This may be the only way to get Riley back," she discreetly added.

My heart sank with those words. I was so scared, but I had to do it. We had to save Riley.

***

"Sit back, relax, and concentrate only on my voice." Madam began slowly and methodically as she raised the ruby stone into view and said, "Watch the stone and just relax. Let your body go. You feel weak, you feel tired, and all you want to do is rest."

I couldn't help but close my eyes. Madam's voice was so soothing. I began to yawn like I hadn't slept in ten years and all I wanted to do was sleep. I felt my body give in as I leaned back into my chair.

"That's good, my child. Now, we're going back. Come with me, Jenny. We're going back now, follow my voice… You're twenty… Now you're fifteen … Now twelve … Eleven … Ten … Nine … Eight … You're seven years old, Jenny. Where are you?" Madam asked. "What do you see?" When she didn't get an answer, she looked at Nichols worriedly.

I turned restless in my chair and started crying out, "No please, it hurts. I promise I'll be good. I won't get into Auntie's makeup no more, please no."

"Jenny, where are you?" Madam asked again. "What do you see? Don't worry, they can't hurt you. Just tell us what you see."

I calmed with Madam's reassuring words and looked around me. "I see my uncle with the belt, and I see Auntie leaving. Why does she leave me? Why doesn't she stop him? I'm a good girl," I cried.

"Jenny? Where are your grandparents?"

"Granny says I can't come back no more cause of the bad man," I said, squirming in my chair like a little child.

"Jenny? Tell me about the bad man," Madam said.

"The bad man is bad. He's mean, and he hits granny, and he stole my dolly. He said I couldn't have my dolly 'til I learn to be good. I am a good girl." I began crying. "I want my dolly. Give me my dolly." The tears streamed down my face. My face turned to terror and I started screaming, "No, no please. Don't take my dolly down there. No, please, she'll be scared. It's dark, and it smells bad." I cried and turned in my chair as if I were wrestling with the devil.

"Can you tell me anything else about the bad man? What does the bad man look like?" Madam dug deeper. "Is the bad man Joseph? What does Joseph do to you?" Madam didn't know what else to say. I didn't seem to be responding as someone normally does under hypnosis, and she was getting frightened.

"No, I don't like the bad man. No, I don't want to see the bad man. He stole my dolly."

"Okay, okay," Madam reassured, "no bad man here. Now Jenny, I want you to concentrate on my voice again and follow me. We're going to a different day. You can feel the sun on your face. The weather is nice and warm with a soft, cool breeze coming off the ocean. You are by the cliff. You are at Willow's Dawn and its summertime, the last day you spent here. Are you there with me, Jenny?" she asked softly. "What do you see?"

"I see Granny and Joseph on the veranda," I said, smiling.

Nichols looked at Madam and mouthed, "Joseph?"

Madam shook her head. She didn't understand either. "Tell me what they are doing while sitting there."

I smiled and giggled. "They're laughing, silly. They love watching me dance, and they think I'm funny," I said, giggling some more in an innocent child's voice.

"Where's your grandfather? Is he laughing, too?" she asked.

I stopped laughing and a glazed look came over my face. "No, he doesn't think I'm funny. He thinks I'm bad."

The table started moving and the cellar door started shaking. Madam looked at Nichols, and he was as white as a sheet. "Stop her, wake her up," he said. Madam put up her hand to silence him.

I began to get mad, and my voice raised into a yell over the noise the table and door were making. "I'm not bad. He's bad. He's a bad man! He killed Joseph, and now he's going to kill you!" I screamed as the cellar door flew open.

The wind came up from the cellar and blew out the candles. The pentagram was gone.

Madam tried to wake me, but the wind drowned out Madam's voice. The table rocked back and forth. She started screaming as loud as her old lungs would allow, "Jenny, when I count to three, you will wake up." The wind was so strong, it almost blew them over. It lifted the table and threw it across the room where it shattered the window. The glass from it came flying at us as Madam and Nichols tried to duck.

"ONE…TWO…THREE!"

All went silent. When I opened my eyes and looked around, I didn't know what to say. They seemed so somber.

"Jenny? Is that you?" Madam asked.

"Yes, what happened? Did I remember?" I asked as I scanned the debris that was once my kitchen.

"Yes, you did fine child. You did fine," she said to me.

I looked at Nichols as he sat across the table from me, all the color gone from his face, so scared and fragile. He was a far cry from the man I had seen earlier. He sat there motionless, unable to speak. He was so scared. Scared for me, scared for Riley, and scared for himself.

***

After all of the excitement wore down, we swept up the broken glass and turned the table back upright. Then, we sat down to relive what had happened while I was under.

After hearing it all, I remembered everything not just the hypnosis, but everything from everywhere, and anything that had ever happened, past and present. I had suppressed all the bad memories that I had, all of the torment, all of the pain.

"I thought all of it was just a bad dream, the house forcing these crazy things into my mind," I said sadly. "Who knew my grandfather could be capable of such a horrid thing." I placed my hands over my face and cried.

Madam softly put her hand on mine. "What do you mean, sweetheart?" she said in a quiet voice.

I just sat there and shook my head in disbelief. *No wonder Social Services wouldn't let me come back to Willow's Dawn*, I thought.

"My grandfather was so jealous of Joseph," I started.

"Joseph? You mean JD," Nichols said.

"No. Well, yes. My grandmother and I called him Joseph. My grandfather called him JD. He hated the fact that he was a good, decent man. More so, he hated that granny and I loved him so much. Joseph played with me all the time. It was better than having a best friend. I had a grown-up who understood me."

I sat with a distant look on my face, recalling all of the fun times I had. But, as I slowly remembered the darkness of my grandfather, all of the fun faded away.

"My grandfather would catch me upstairs at night when I was getting ready for bed and sit and tell me what a horrible person JD was. He said that I should never, ever be alone with him, that he would do unspeakable things to me. Then, my granny would come in and yell at him to stop filling my head with such nonsense, and he'd stand up and storm out. One night, not long before I left Willow's Dawn for good, he said, 'One day, I will prove myself right, and then heaven help you both.' We didn't pay any attention to him. He was always talking down Joseph like that."

I hid my face in my hands again and started crying. "But then one day I was out by the veranda, and I was playing and spinning back and forth, around and around, and I was making myself dizzy. Just like a kid does."

Madam and Nichols sat captivated by my account as I stopped to catch my breath to continue. "Well, I got a little too close to the edge, and I heard Joseph yell my name. My grandfather came running at me like a mad man, and Joseph went running after him. I heard my grandfather yell out, 'I ought to push her. That'll teach her a lesson!' Then I heard Joseph yell, 'Please Mister, don't do it,' and Joseph lunged for me. My grandfather lunged at him and ended up pushing me right over the side of the cliff."

I was crying so hard at this point I almost couldn't be understood. "The only thing is that Joseph's face was the last face I saw. So, I truly thought he was the one who pushed me and that my grandfather was right all of those years. Of course, after what it looked like, my grandmother believed him, too. Social Services came to the hospital, and I told them that Joseph had pushed me over the edge. I was never allowed back at Willow's Dawn. I didn't know what to believe. I couldn't believe Joseph had done it and I heard my grandfather say he was going to push me, but everyone was telling me Joseph did it."

They both sat quietly, just staring at me not knowing what to say. What was there to say? I had been lied to and deceived. One of the only people who ever loved me unconditionally died thinking I thought the worst of him. Poor, pitiful Joseph. What had I done? I started crying again. My broken heart would never heal. How would I ever say I was sorry? How would he ever forgive me? Then, I remembered the crime scene and what Nichols had told me the night they had searched the house for Joseph.

"I still don't understand. Didn't you say that Joseph left a note that he killed my grandparents? How do you explain that?" I asked. "What happened that night, and why do I dream about it? I wasn't even there. It was three weeks after the accident, and I was still in the hospital from the fall."

Madam raised her head and said, "That is something Joseph is going to have to tell us."

She pulled two tablecloths, one black and one white, out of her bag and placed the white one on the table.

"What's with the different colors?" I asked.

"Well, the white cloth is to contact peaceful spirits, the black for evil. If you remember, I explained it's all about good versus evil, Heaven versus Hell." And with that, she relit the candles for our séance.

CHAPTER TEN

Once again, the room was lit with the eerie glow of the candle's light, shadows playing on the walls like demons beckoning us to follow them. It was almost unimaginable that we were even sitting here doing this after the last round. It had to go on, but what happens if we fail? What happens if something goes wrong? As if Madam was reading my mind, she reached out and squeezed my hand as if to say, "relax." Nichols and I sat still until she was ready to begin.

"Please join hands." she said. "We need to try to make contact with Joseph and get him out of the attic. If he faces and fights the evil that is within this house, then we can trap it and set Joseph free."

We all joined hands and looked at one another. "Are we ready?" she asked.

I could tell by the sweat building up between Nichols' and my hand that he was not ready. I didn't know if he would be able to go through with this. He looked so afraid, like a little boy. But if this didn't turn him into a man, nothing would. We both looked at Madam and nodded.

"Good, please stay calm and seated at all times. Outbursts will upset the spirits, and it can also drive them away. Let us begin," she said, lowering her head. "Everyone take a few breaths in through your nose and out through your mouth. This will help you relax and be susceptible to welcoming the spirit."

She looked at Nichols and I until she was satisfied.

"Now close your eyes and repeat after me: Joseph, we ask that you commune with us and move among us. Again," she said, nodding. "Joseph, we ask that you commune with us and move among us."

We repeated this over and over again until we noticed the temperature change in the room. I wanted to grab my sweater but knew I couldn't break the circle.

"Joseph? Are you with us?" Madam asked. "Joseph, if you are here with us, please rap three times."

We sat silently for what seemed like an eternity until we heard three faint raps. Madam took a deep breath and proceeded.

"Joseph, thank you for coming to speak with us. I'm going to be asking you a few simple yes-or-no questions. Please respond with one rap for yes or two raps for no. Will that be alright with you, Joseph?"

We waited for the raps but heard nothing.

"Joseph, we are not here to cause you any harm. I have Jenny here with me. Do you remember Jenny? She knows you didn't hurt her. She has found out the truth. We want to help you and we want you to help us. Joseph, are you still with us?"

Still, nothing but silence.

Madam sighed deeply. "Joseph, Jenny's grandfather has come back and he's trying to hurt her again. We need your help."

A cold burst of wind ripped through the kitchen and I screamed in fright. "Hush, my child, and remember it's only Joseph," she said, patting my hand.

The curtains that hung on the kitchen door fell to the floor as glasses that were in the cabinets came flying out. We ducked to miss them as they crashed to the floor all around us, and the back door swung violently in the wind.

Madam yelled over the noise, "Joseph, he won't hurt her if you help us! You can protect her this time, but we need you. You can stop it before it happens."

The wind slowly died down and all became quiet again.

"Joseph, I would like to ask you a few questions. Will that be alright?" she repeated.

This time, before she even finished her words, we heard one rap from a distance. Madam nodded her head to us and smiled. It was Joseph's love and the need to take care of me that brought him out to us, and with him, we would be rid of the evil once and for all.

"Are you JD, the caretaker of Willow's Dawn?" she started.

Joseph rapped once.

"Do you remember playing with Jenny when she was a little girl?"

Joseph rapped once, again.

"Joseph, do you remember that day at the edge of the cliff?"

Joseph didn't respond.

"Joseph, I need you to remember. This is very important. We don't have to talk about it, just answer a couple of questions."

Joseph finally rapped once.

"Okay. After Jenny went to the hospital, did she ever return to the house after that?"

Joseph rapped twice. *No.*

"Do you know where Riley is?"

Joseph rapped once again. *Yes.*

"Joseph? We need to find out what happened the night you killed yourself."

Joseph rapped twice, and then twice more.

"Joseph? No, what? No, you don't want to talk about it?"

Joseph rapped twice again.

Madam looked at Nichols and me and said, "Okay, this is getting confusing,"

Joseph rapped once and we all kind of let out an amused but scared chuckle.

"I'm going to see if he will step inside me so you," she said looking at me, "can ask him the rest of the questions. It will be easier on all of us."

I looked at Madam in disbelief. "Do you think that's a good idea? What if something goes wrong?" I was very concerned at this point that the house might have been tricking us again. What if it wasn't Joseph? What if it was my grandfather tricking us?

"No, it will be fine. I can feel Joseph's presence, and he won't let anything harm us."

Madam sounded convinced, but I was very unsure. I couldn't get the thought of Nichols standing in my closet with the ax out of my head. If my grandfather was capable of doing that, what else would he do?

"I will only agree to this if you are completely sure, Madam," I said to all of them.

Nichols looked at Madam with a plea in his eyes. "Jenny's right. I don't think this is a good idea. I have a bad feeling about this," he stuttered.

"Now, now, look who's become the physic," Madam said very callously. "Look, we can do this my way, or your partner can be lost forever. Your call."

Madam sat for the longest time just staring at Nichols. Neither one of them would blink.

"Well?" she blurted out and scared Nichols as he almost fell off his chair, breaking the circle.

"Okay, fine. We'll do it," he said. "Let's just get on with it. I'm starting to get a headache."

"Sometimes I'm delighted I don't live in this town. I'm sure your streets are extremely safe," Madam said with a huff and a grunt.

Nichols just stared at Madam, not knowing what to say. When he finally found his voice, all he could mutter was, "What do you mean by that?"

"It means, dear boy, that you are a spineless, chickenhearted kid who doesn't have the right to wear a badge. Stand up for something for once in your life and be a man for Christ's sake. Take the bull by the horns and be something, and don't just wait for others to do it for you." Madam was so frustrated you could see the veins pulsing in her forehead. "I am here to do what I can to protect you from this house. We must get your partner back and if you don't want to participate, then maybe you should go."

"Please, both of you stop. This isn't helping anyone, and you're just going to upset Joseph," I said as Joseph rapped once. "See." I smiled.

They both sat at the table with their heads hung low. "Well, is anyone going to say anything?" I asked.

Madam looked up and said, "Joseph, would you like to move into me and use my voice and my body as yours?" Joseph rapped once, and Madam hung her head down and waited for the transformation to take place.

After a moment or two, Madam's right arm started to shake. I looked at Nichols and he nodded his head as if it were normal. Then, she slowly raised her head and looked at us, almost as if passing straight through our bodies to the wall behind us, and with a sudden jerk, her head kicked back as her eyeballs rolled into the back of her head.

I went to stand up to break the circle, but Nichols held me down and mouthed the words, "Just wait."

Madam's head turned upright once more, this time looking straight at me, and in a tone I hadn't heard for many years, she said, "Jennifer, sweetheart, so good to see ya, child." She spoke in Joseph's sweet, southern accent. My tears began to flow freely. There was so much love in just that one sentence. How good it was to hear his words again.

I sniffled. "Hello Joseph. I'm so sorry," I said, hanging my head in shame.

"No, child. Don't go worrying your pretty lil' head about such things," he said, patting my hand.

I smiled back at him for his kind words and said, "Joseph? I need to ask you a few questions, is that alright?"

"Yes, ma'am. You go on ahead, ask old Joseph anything," he said sweetly.

"Is Riley safe?" I hadn't thought that it would be my first question, but it slipped out before I had a chance to think about it.

"Of course he is, child. I answered that one for ya upstairs." He smiled as he spoke.

It was bizarre to see Madam sitting before me talking as one of my oldest friends. It almost made me want to giggle.

I smiled. "So that was you upstairs," I said more as a statement than a question. "Thank you for saving me from Nichols. If it wasn't for you, I would be dead."

The look on Joseph's face stopped me from smiling and scared me a bit. I almost wanted to take back what I had said.

"Nah ma'am, that wasn't Nichols. That was pure evil, and helping you is what I'm here to do," he said with a wink. "Anyway, he couldn't have hurt you. The evil wasn't strong enough then, but now, now I fear he has gotten very much stronger."

"What is in the cellar, Joseph?" I asked abruptly but cautiously.

"Ma'am, you don't wanna go down there. Nothing good can come of it.

That's where he is, the bad man."

Those words cut straight through me. Those were my words, the words I used to describe all of the evil memories I had of my grandfather, the bad man. "My grandfather?" I asked.

"Yes, ma'am. He's there too, so don't you be going down there. Nothing good can come of it. Nothing I tell you, nothing."

Joseph started fidgeting in his chair like the bottom was sending electrical shocks straight through him. I knew he was getting stressed out and was beginning to fear for my safety, but I needed to calm him down before we lost him.

"I'm not going down there, Joseph. I'm staying right here with you." I smiled and squeezed his hand, then he eased back a little in the chair.

"Promise me, girl, you won't go down there," he said to me accusingly.

"No, I'll stay right here, Joseph," I lied. I had every intention of going down there and getting Riley. I knew he was there, and I wanted him back.

"Joseph? I want to talk about that night, the night you killed yourself," I started.

"Now I already told y'all that I didn't go killing myself!" he shouted.

"Then tell me what happened." I smiled, hoping to ease him into telling us.

Joseph began to have tears in his eyes. "Do I got to?" he asked.

"It would help us if you did. I love my house and I want to make Willow's Dawn safe again, but I need you to help me put the evil to rest. In return, you'll be at rest, too."

Joseph looked at me and started shaking his head.

"I don't wanna leave ya, Missy. I wanna stay here at Willow's Dawn. She's my home and she needs me. *You* need me," he protested.

I sighed. "We'll talk about that, but right now we need to talk about that night." I nodded my head for him to continue.

"Yes, I understand." He hung his head down for a minute before he continued.

"Well, it all started as a normal night. Missus had just finished baking one of her famous sweet apple pies, and Mister was up in his office working. I never rightly understood what he did up there 'til all hours of the night, you know being retired and all. But he'd work a little upstairs, then go down to the cellar and work a little more down there. I always thought he was trying to finish her up, but whenever I'd go down there, it always looked the same. Mister and Missus would fight like cats and dogs about that place. Neither one of us knew what could be taking him so long getting it done and all. He'd always say that if you want it safe, you have to do it right. Weird, old man is what he was," he said with a huff. He took a deep breath and slowly looked around the kitchen and behind him at the cellar door.

"Ya know, I always thought it funny. He'd be down there all talking to himself and stuff, yell at the walls and saying some bizarre stuff. Then that night," he lowered his head and brought his voice down to a whisper, "I heard him talking, so I sneaked down there all quiet like, ya know, so he wouldn't know I was there. Well, I heard someone - or better than that, something talk to him. Didn't know much about what they said, but I heard Mister saying stuff like, 'he's gonna kill me and the Missus.'"

The cellar door started rattling again. I looked at Nichols with a look of desperation, wanting to stop this. Joseph continued his story.

"Well, I was so scared that I went and told the Missus what I'd heard, but she wouldn't believe me. She still thought I was the one that tried to harm you Missy, and it wasn't me. Well, she got furious at me and told me to go to my room, so I went knowing that if I didn't, Mister would be even madder." He stopped and put his face in his hands, crying and shaking. "She didn't even see it coming," he said as the tears started flowing more frequently. "Poor, poor Miss Elouise. She didn't even see it coming, and I wasn't there to help her. I wasn't there to protect her. Why did I go…why did I go?" He stopped for a moment, and the cellar door became quiet.

"You know, he's listening to us. He's coming…I can feel him."

As Joseph spoke, every hair on the back of my neck stood erect. If he was right, we could all die tonight. I didn't know what to do. Should I stop it and tell him to go in peace, or should I take the chance that Joseph was strong enough to fight him off? I was so confused. I could tell by the look on Nichols's face that it was my call, that I was the only one who could do anything right now. I chose to save Riley.

"Please, Joseph. Finish telling us about that night."

Joseph looked around the room again and then apprehensively continued his story. "I was out at the barn sitting on my bunk when I heard this noise coming from outside the door. It wasn't like footsteps or anything I'd ever heard before. It was like a gush of wind walking through the trees. I swore I heard them talking the trees, that is. They were crying and whispering. It was the strangest dang thing I'd ever heard. When I stepped out of the doorway, Mister came up behind me and grabbed me by my neck. I couldn't breathe, Missy. I was so dab gummed scared." Joseph stopped to wipe the tears out of his eyes and took a deep breath.

From behind him, it looked like the doorknob on the cellar door was turning, but I couldn't concentrate on it long enough to be sure. Something wanted out of there, and our séance wasn't letting it go. In a way, I felt reassured by this thought. But then again, how mad will it be when it finally did get out?

"Well, Mister pushed me towards the house, saying he wanted to show me something. It started storming real, real bad, almost like it just fell out of the sky with no warning or nothing. When we got through the kitchen door, I noticed all the lights were out. The cellar door was open and there was this smell, Ma'am. It smelled just like those foxes smelled after I had to kill 'em and throw 'em out back in the sun to dry. It reeked just like that. Then, he threw me down on the kitchen floor and kicked me real good in the stomach and told me to get up and called me a bad, bad, name. Ma'am, that hurt worse than the blow in my belly. Ain't no one ever call me that before. I just didn't know what had gotten into the old Mister. Still, I stumbled to my feet and he pushed me into the living room where the sweet Missus was and…"

The cellar door was rocking with such force, Joseph was almost afraid to go on. We were all scared and didn't know what would happen next.

"And she was just lying there all covered in blood, and there was blood all over the walls, and the smell, the smell was so unbearable," he said, starting to weep.

I shifted in my chair nervously as I looked from Joseph to the door and said, "Go on, Joseph, we have to do this. You have to get it out."

"He threw me down onto the poor Missus and said, 'See, look what you made me do,' and hit me in the back with something metal, like a stick or something, and kept poking at me 'til I was all rolled around in the poor Missus' blood. I could feel the warmth of it on my skin, and it had a lovely smell. I wasn't sure if I'd imagined it or if it was real. It felt warm and sticky on my face. After old Mister finished with it, he put a paper in my hand and told me to write out how I killed 'em. Ma'am, I swear I didn't do it. Then, he slapped me upside my head with that metal stick and everything went black. Next thing I knew, I was hung up in the cellar and all these police officers were poking their noses everywhere. I tried to holler at them, but they wouldn't hear me. But I heard 'em say that I'd killed myself after I'd killed the Mister and Missus. But Missy, I didn't do it I tell you, I didn't. I tried to get them to help me. I even wrote it out all nice like on the wall, but they didn't care."

Joseph was sobbing uncontrollably at this point, and I didn't know what to say. I knew he didn't do it, but then again, if he didn't know, who killed my grandfather?

"Joseph, I believe you, I do. But if my grandfather killed you, then who killed him?"

I thought the cellar door was going to fly off its hinges as it rocked back and forth looking as if it could burst open at any minute. The noise was almost deafening as I watched Joseph rock back and forth in his chair like a child.

"Joseph?" I yelled.

The wind from out of nowhere seemed to pick up again. The kitchen was so cold that Joseph was forming little bits of ice on his eyebrows. I stuttered from the cold as I tried to continue my quest.

"If you didn't kill Granddad, then who did?"

Joseph wouldn't answer me, but I could hear Nichols yelling at me to stop and end this madness. I pressed on. I had to know.

"Joseph, answer me! Who killed my grandfather?" I yelled, shaking him by the hand as I held on tight. "Tell me!" I screamed.

Joseph looked up at me and with a horrified look on his face, then stood up, breaking the circle.

"This HOUSE!" he screamed.

The cellar door flew open, and Joseph turned as the spirit attacked him. I screamed and jumped away from the table as Nichols grabbed me and pulled me into safety.

"Madam!" I screamed and lunged for her.

Nichols pulled me back as the spirit grabbed Joseph and flew across the room, sending the table and all the candles flying. One of the candles landed on the fallen curtain, which then caught on fire. Joseph turned and noticed the flames and Madam Zola's body, where she had fallen to the floor with a thump as Joseph's spirit and the house wrestled violently.

Nichols grabbed me and hoisted me over his shoulder while I screamed and cried for Madam and Riley. He ran with me out the front door and dropped me in the driveway by his car.

"Here," he said, handing me his cell phone. "Call 911. I'm going back in to get Madam."

I screamed at him to go to the cellar and get Riley and Baby also, but he couldn't hear me over the commotion going on from inside the house, now raging with fire.

***

The fire had already grown stronger as Nichols made his way through the front door. He thought he heard Jenny scream something, but his adrenaline was pumping so hard it didn't register in enough time for him to stop.

The smoke filled his lungs the moment he walked through the door.

"Madam? Can you hear me?" he yelled. "Where are you?"

He dropped down to his knees to get away from the smoke and began crawling towards the kitchen entryway. The flames were out of control, so he didn't know how he would be able to reach Madam, and even if he did, she would surely be dead. He made contact with the sidewall, where he had encountered the blood from that very first night. He cringed at the thought of touching it, but he had to get to Madam and prove to her that he could do something right.

As he made his way further into the house, he stopped and stared in pure amazement. Nichols could see the figures of the two spirits wrestling, hovering high in the air over the now glowing pentagram. He tried to hide but was mesmerized by the glowing lesions. The flames danced off of them like fire licking the wood on a cold winter's night. Right below them laid

Madam's lifeless body. Nichols let out a cry. After everything she had done, how could it end this way? He sat there wondering what to do next, as he was too scared to move. The flames were standing tall like a gate of fire between him and Madam. How would he get to her? He was about to turn and make his way back out when he heard the voice of Joseph once again, but this time powerful and demanding. He turned towards the sound and saw Joseph with his hands around what must have been the grandfather's neck.

"I command the to be gone!" Joseph screamed.

Nichols caught a movement out of the corner of his eye. It was the Ouija board rocking, lifting off of the floor.

"I command the to be gone!" he yelled again and threw the spirit towards the Ouija board.

Nichols watched as the spirit disappeared into the board with a scream of anguish louder than he had ever heard before, and then all went silent.

Joseph looked at Nichols and made a parting motion with his arms, and the fire and smoke made way to Madam's body. While Nichols rushed over and hoisted Madam up and over his shoulders, he grabbed the Ouija board and made his way to the front door. He stopped and turned around to tell Joseph, "Thank you," but Joseph was nowhere to be seen.

***

I put the phone down after calling for help and sat and stared at the front door. I couldn't see anything, no signs of life. I waited a few more minutes, and then stood up in a panic. It was taking too long, something was wrong.

"Oh god, this isn't happening!" I screamed as I limped as fast as I could for the entrance and to Nichols carrying Madam's lifeless body.

"Noooo!" I cried, laying Madam down by his car.

"Did you call 911?" he asked.

"Yes, they should be here soon," I said, cradling her softly. "What happened while you were in there? Did you see Riley?"

I was trying to hold back my tears, as so much had happened in the last few weeks, I felt like a china doll ready to break. How could it end this way? How could I have let this happen? I should have stopped it.

Nichols swiped my hair out of my face and softly said, "I'm so sorry, Jenny, but I think Riley's gone. The kitchen and the cellar are both engulfed in flames. There's no way anyone could have survived that, but Joseph did it. I do have the Ouija board and the evil spirit is trapped, so we can bury it in the morning."

I didn't care about that anymore. It was all for nothing. Riley was gone. I had failed him.

Madam opened her eyes and smiled. "No child, you haven't failed. We won," she said while looking at me. Then she grabbed Nichols hand. "What a brave man you are," she said, closing her eyes as her life force left her body.

***

It was daybreak before the last of the fire was put out. We both sat lifeless in silence as we watched the fire department pack everything up and roll out of the driveway. The house would survive, but I would need to remodel the kitchen because it and the cellar were destroyed. All that was left was an open hole with concrete walls. They found no remains. They said he probably got out and they would call again in the afternoon. They pretended to care.

The cause of the fire was determined to be a candle that got knocked over. The police didn't understand the earthquake destruction that had occurred on it beforehand, though. Nichols and I just looked at each other, not knowing what to tell them. We'd surely be sent to the asylum if we told the truth.

After everyone was gone, Nichols and I went to the back of the house out by the veranda, where he dug a deep hole and got the chainsaw from his trunk. "So, this will work, right?" I asked. He just looked at me and shrugged his shoulders.

"It's what Madam said to do," he said as he placed the broken pieces into the ground, set it on fire, and piled the dirt on top.

"Should we say a blessing or something? You know, like they do at funerals?" I asked.

"I thought you didn't believe in God."

I looked at him and nodded, "I do now. I've seen it. I've seen Hell and what is a Hell without a Heaven, and what is Heaven without a God." I turned, hung my head down low, and walked to the edge of the cliff. How much I wanted just to jump and end all of the pain I was feeling, just spread my wings and fly. I opened my arms and held them out away from my side and slowly felt myself going forward. My world started spinning as I got dizzier and started to fall, but in a moment's notice, something grabbed me from behind and stopped me. I heard a voice whispering in my ear, "Now, now Miss Jennifer. You don't want to be doing something like that." I was so beaten and worn down, my head collapsed on to Joseph's head and thought, *just let me go*.

"Look down, child. What do you see?"

I looked down and began crying.

"Now, you don't think old Joseph would let anything happen now, do you?" Joseph held my body just over the edge of the cliff, and Baby looked up and barked at me. She was lying on the rocks next to Riley's body.

"Nichols!" I screamed. "It's Riley!"

"What?" he yelled, running over and looking over the edge. "But how? And how did you know?" he looked at me, confused as ever.

I smiled and said, "Joseph showed me."

"Joseph? Well, I'll be damned," he said with a smile on his face, looking back at the shell of a house.

"No, you be blessed," I said, winking at him.

***

When we finally had Baby and Riley pulled to safety, Riley still had a strong heartbeat. We couldn't believe it. If only Madam was here to share our joy.

"Don't think about that," Nichols said. "Remember, she already knew. She told you we won."

I remembered her words and smiled, "Yeah, I guess she did."

Riley moaned a little and looked up at Nichols and me. "What happened? Did I catch the bad guy?" he asked with a smile.

I softly stroked his cheek and said, "Yes, baby. You got the bad guy."

EPILOGUE

Days, weeks, years had passed since our fire at Willow's Dawn. I chose to stay through it all, since it was, in fact, my home. And I would stay, if not, just to protect her.

The construction took six months and a day before all the noises and bumps stopped. Even then on stormy nights, I could still hear noises coming from the attic.

Joseph decided to stay, said he wouldn't leave. The house needed him, and so did I. I agreed.

As I stood at the edge of the cliff, I could feel the fresh, autumn air flowing through my hair as I looked out towards the ocean. The wind whipped through my dress as a sense of peace washed over me. I heard from the distance someone call my name. I turned around and saw it was Riley smiling and waving to me from the veranda. I waved back as he started walking towards me. I could see the wind blow through his white work shirt. I closed my eyes and turned back towards the sea. I thanked God for all the happiness that I have in my life. As Riley approached me, I felt his arms encircle me like a perfect vine to its rose. I could feel his breath on my neck and in my ear the whisper of his loving words as he placed his hand on my swelling belly and kissed my cheek. "So how are my girls?" he asked.

I smiled and rested my head against his shoulder as he kissed my forehead. "I felt her move today," I said proudly. I grabbed his arm that was around me and held him tight.

I had finally found everything I had always wanted: love, security, and faith.

END

* * *

Thank you for reading my first book. I hope you enjoyed it. If you did, please think about leaving a review on Amazon. Every review counts. Follow me to find out when my next book will be released. Thank you again.

https://distractionsinmyhead.com
https://www.facebook.com/GoldieAnnBrand/
https://www.instagram.com/distractionsinmyhead/
https://twitter.com/GoldieannB

ABOUT THE AUTHOR

GoldieAnn Brand has been writing horror ever since she read her first Stephen King book at ten years old. She believes everything she writes can be traced back to the moment of revelation. She lives in sunny Florida with her husband and many assortments of animals. She enjoys; kayaking, rock climbing, diving. When she's not writing, you can find her traveling the country and blogging about her adventures.

Printed in Dunstable, United Kingdom